MATTHEW LIVINGSTON

AND

THE MILLIONAIRE MURDER

By

Marco Conelli

iUniverse, Inc.
New York   Bloomington

Matthew Livingston and the Millionaire Murder

iUniverse books may be ordered through booksellers or by contacting:

iUniverse
1663 Liberty Drive
Bloomington, IN 47403
www.iuniverse.com
1-800-Authors (1-800-288-4677)

*Because of the dynamic nature of the Internet, any Web addresses or
links contained in this book may have changed since publication and
may no longer be valid. The views expressed in this work are solely those
of the author and do not necessarily reflect the views of the publisher,
and the publisher hereby disclaims any responsibility for them.*

ISBN: 978-1-4401-2347-4 (pbk)
ISBN: 978-1-4401-2348-1 (ebk)

Printed in the United States of America

iUniverse rev. date: 3/18/2009

CHAPTER 1.

WHEN IN DOUBT, GET OUT!

"Now this was just plain wrong!"

I clutched the 8 & ½ by 11 inch piece of white paper and stared at it in disbelief. There were a few instructions on it and a contact phone number. I wasn't even aware that the first floor classroom, which served as the office for the school newspaper staff, had emptied. Now I didn't even have anyone to complain to.

The other reporter's assignments were pinned to a bulletin board at the front of the room. Stephen Ross, senior editor, was covering game seven of the basketball playoffs, serious do or die stuff. Shelley Coverdale, alternate senior editor, was called in to handle the story about the graffiti some one sprayed on the school's front wall. Yours truly Dennis Sommers, junior editor, had to interview some old spud named Malcom Everest. This rich, primed to croak geezer was donating a chunk of money to our high school to help fund special programs.

The school paper wanted me to get an in-depth story about this relic. Talk about a fun time.

My philosophy was when presented with a distasteful assignment; handle it as quick as possible, don't procrastinate. Practicing what I preach, I used the phone in the empty classroom and dialed the number on the assignment sheet. Everest answered and he said I could see him after school. Using one of my laptops, the one I usually keep in my locker, I went online and put his name in a search engine. There were a lot of news articles about this guy. I scanned the headlines. I wanted to know a bit about him before our interview. There were also a good number of pictures of the old timer. He was quite distinguished looking. At two p.m., when my eighth period class ended, I headed off in the direction of his home.

Strand Street was a beauty. Houses stood as high as the eye could stretch. I was aware Mr. Everest was quite wealthy but the site of his extravagant estate reassured me that he wasn't about to starve. I stopped short in front of the magnificent structure and examined my appearance. I quickly tucked my black t-shirt into my pants and straightened out my rumpled denim jacket. Running my hand through my recently gelled blond hair I realized no power on earth was going to make it spike. I walked slowly up the marble walkway and climbed the stoop.

Aiming my index finger at the doorbell I pressed it. I could hear the ringing echo inside the house. Loud as it was it drew my attention to the fact that the front door was slightly open. My neck let out a slight creak as I shifted my head from right to left to make certain I was alone. Confident that I was, I pressed it again. A chill in the afternoon air hit my bones like an Arctic breeze. I clutched the ends of my denim jacket closer to my body which I swore was going to undertake a diet, and soon!

I didn't hear a sound emanating from the house and suddenly realized my left hand was grasping the silver handle of the screen door. I opened it and pushed lightly on the hinged oak door behind it. It swung wide open revealing a finely furnished living room. I stepped inside and my nostrils immediately protested. A burnt odor consumed the air. At first I thought something got overcooked, but no! Ash and soot were blowing across the floor courtesy of the draft coming from the open front door. I followed a trail of it to a small room adjacent to the living room. Stepping inside it I saw Malcom Everest sprawled out on the floor, dead as a doornail.

A numb sensation overcame my arms and legs. The only window in the room was shattered. Books, a bookshelf, and an entire computer system were charred and scattered across the floor. The wall area, over the window, was black as burnt toast. I turned to run!

It was a short trip because I crashed right into the barrel chest of a man in an overcoat and a tie. His vice like hands clasped my shoulders, dragged me into the hall, and slammed me face first against a wall. The impact spilled several hanging picture frames to the floor. I heard the sound of people racing into the house and it appeared they were heading into the room where Malcom Everest's corpse lay. It was then that I realized that the stampede I was hearing was the police. Two uniformed officers led the charge.

A brutish voice called out, "We got a stiff in here! Looks like something blew him and part of this room up."

A booming noise rang out as the ape who was holding me spun me around and planted my back against the wall. My bones shook violently. I looked up and saw another barrel chest, suit wearing figure of authority. This guy looked like he just chewed a box of brass nails for lunch. He stood about 6' 3" and his crew cut hair made his head look like it was carved out of butter. He was mangling a toothpick between his teeth. He methodically removed it and flipped it in my direction. Gross!

"You want to tell us what you're doing here?" he asked very arrogantly.

I didn't like the picture that was being painted. The cop that was still grasping my shoulder asked, "What's you're name kid?"

Searching for my voice I nervously replied, "Dennis Sommers."

"Where do you live, Sommers?"

"Twenty Five Brenner Lane."

The crew cut cop stepped closer and said, "We received a call from a neighbor. They stated they heard a loud noise come from this address and a portly young man in a denim jacket entering the premises."

I needed to rectify this and quick! "No. I was supposed to interview Mr. Everest for my school's newspaper." My fingers shimmered through my jacket pocket and found the assignment sheet. I thrust it in the cop's direction.

Snatching it out of my hand the other officer frisked my immediate area.

"Sit down kid," he said after he read the assignment sheet. "Get comfortable, you're going to be here a while."

The other guy finally released his grip on me. He followed his partner into the room where Everest's body was. From what I could tell the two uniformed officers were in there as well.

I was sitting on Everest's couch and after a moment I realized I was alone. I didn't like this situation one bit. My stomach turned to sour milk and I launched myself off the couch and out the front door. I don't think my feet ever touched the floor. I tore across Everest's front lawn and down the block. My jacket was flapping against my back so hard I thought I was going to take flight. I hit the corner of Pike street and stopped to suck air into my lungs. Once I achieved oxygen intake I started to run again. Perspiration danced across my face as I ran another block and a half and had to quickly think where I was going to go. These cops had my home address, I couldn't go there. In my panicked state I realized I turned onto Baskerville Street. It was then that I saw the familiar home of Matthew Livingston. I made a bee line for the garage.

CHAPTER 2.

SEEMED LIKE A GOOD IDEA AT THE TIME.

The detached garage, split leveled on the inside, always gave me the creeps. The silence swallowed me as I stepped inside. I put my foot down on the first step as I headed up to the loft. A soft squeak rose through the quiet surroundings. I made my way up and gazed at the familiar sites. The old yellow sofa and the large wooden wheel sat in their familiar places. The latter served as a combination coffee table, desk, and foot rest. I remembered clearly the conversations we had and the plotting we did in this very room. We rescued one of our high school peers from a maniacal religious cult while coming to the aid of a friend who was burglarized. A memoir I had since referred to as *the Prison of Souls*. Looking around, I wasn't sure if Matthew was here.

"Hey Matt," I called in the direction of the heavy black curtain that sectioned off the back of the loft.

"Hey Matt, are you in there?"

There was a quiet moment and then like a band of rattle snakes on the prowl a loud hiss consumed the air. Smoke enveloped the area where I was standing.

I barely had time to cough when the black curtain flew back. Another gust of smoke wrapped around the loft and then he appeared.

The white laboratory coat was draped across his shoulders in perfect symmetry. His hands were in tan, industrial sized workman's gloves. The black slacks he wore were meticulously creased down to his matching loafers. The smoke had disappeared and I could better see the stone-like expression on my friend's face. He was motionless at first, but then he pulled the safety goggles off his face and launched them onto the wheel top.

For a minute I thought I saw the devil. Matthew dropped onto the sofa and his facial muscles tied themselves into a knot.

"Something wrong," I asked softly.

He stared straight ahead and replied, "About a week's worth of work has been ruined."

"What happened?"

"The same thing that usually happens," he said quietly.

"What's that?"

"I go to delicately add a highly flammable ingredient to a formula and someone shouts, 'Hey Matt, are you there'."

It took about half a minute and then I got it. He made his point; I did barge in on him. He cast his gaze upon me and asked, "What do you want?"

"I encountered a small problem today."

He stood up and took the white coat off and hung it on a rack next to the curtain. He turned to face me and said, "Well it's quite obvious you ran all the way over here, so it must be important."

I looked at my t-shirt and yes it was wet from perspiration. It wasn't particularly hot out so it was pretty obvious I had been running.

"I noticed you also cut across the North West corner of Pike Street," he added.

I thought to myself for a moment and then got a bit freaked out. How did he know that? I must have been wearing confusion like a hat because he answered my question.

"Your pants," he said again sitting. "The cuffs have fresh clay splattering on them. I know they are digging up the North West corner of Pike Street and that clay is in abundance over there."

I exhaled as if I were blowing out a candle. "Thank you for clearing that up."

He leaned back on the couch and his eyes narrowed forming slits under his thin eye brows.

"I'm waiting," he said coldly.

I gave it to him, verbatim. I started with my day at school and chronicled the whole afternoon that brought me right to his loft. When I finished there was nothing but silence. After a minute or two, he spoke.

"You didn't do anything wrong, so why did you run?"

"I didn't think they were going to believe me and personally I was tired of getting slammed against a wall."

Now this was a first. He actually started to chuckle and asked, "Did they really do that?"

"Yes!"

He swallowed the chuckle and asked, "So at what point in your life did you think it was a good idea to come to my place?"

"Listen! Are you going to help me or not?"

"I will," he replied and looked away. "After I've made certain you didn't kill Malcom Everest."

My eyes almost popped out of my head and I gasped in disbelief.

"What," I shouted with vehemence. "You must be joking!"

"No," he raised his voice in response, "it would be a joke for me to undertake looking into this matter without judging it first!"

I couldn't believe what I was hearing. My own friend doubted me. I stood alone with no witnesses.

"You must go now," he said.

Feeling slightly offended I asked, "What are you going to do?"

He picked his safety glasses off the table and said, "When I feel you need to know that information, I promise to supply you with it."

I left. My pace had slowed considerably. My right foot seemed to be kicking at the road every time I put it forward. I slammed my hands into the pockets of my denim jacket and dropped my head down. It had gotten dark since I was last outside. Dejected, I headed in the direction of home. I reached in the front right pocket of my blue jeans and pulled out my cell phone. I made a call to both my parents, who were at their respective jobs, but they were unavailable. As my sneakers pointed in the direction of Brenner Lane I saw my house. Parked right in front of it was a police car. I wasn't running anymore today. If my own friend Matthew Livingston didn't believe me, why should I bother running? I gave myself up.

CHAPTER 3.

WITHERS AND RILEY

The police station in our town is a two story structure in dire need of some fresh paint. They had me sitting in a small room that reeked of disinfectant. I was handcuffed to a long steel bar that was bolted to the cinder block wall.

So far it was a productive experience. I learned that the two people who dealt with me at Everest's house were detectives. I also learned their names. The one who manhandled me was Detective Withers and the one with the head carved out of butter was Detective Riley. I also learned that the concrete cube I was sitting in was called the interview room. Withers and Riley had detained me for close to an hour. My education didn't end there either. I learned that being sixteen years old, they could only interrogate me in the presence of a guardian. Normally this would be a good thing, but it wasn't. Namely because it meant I had to hang out with this less than dynamic duo until someone claimed me. Riley was sitting right in front of me telling stories of what happens to people my age in jail. Withers was leaning against the two way mirror. Riley's technique was awful. Whenever he intended to put a scare into me he would start yelling. He was trying to prepare me to sing a confession for when and if my folks did show up. They were still unreachable.

I couldn't help but notice that the two detectives were dressed almost identical. They wore the same style suits and ties and both were flashing a ring on their pinky finger.

"Two for one on the suits," I asked tiredly, "or do you guys share?"

Riley, not amused, placed his right foot on the bench I was sitting on and shouted, "I can't question you about the crime yet, but I'll give you the benefit of the doubt. I think you were embarking on a shopping spree in the millionaire's house."

Some benefit of the doubt. I was outraged; I lunged forward and forgot I was restrained to the wall. The handcuff bit into my wrist and I recoiled quickly. Shaking it off, I stared daggers at the two of them.

Both their heads turned quickly toward the only door and I couldn't believe my eyes.

"I'm going to guess that burglaries need to be solved in your statistics department."

The profound statement came from the familiar face framed attractively by long crimson red hair. The emerald eyes were nestled behind steel rimmed glasses perfectly placed on a gorgeous pale complexion. Sandra Small was standing in the doorway of the interview room.

Riley stepped forward to argue as an older man in a brown rumpled suit sporting tobacco stains on his fingers and a face swimming in liver spots entered and announced, "Cut him loose boys, his mouthpiece is here, and he's standing mute."

I figured out that the older man was a supervisor. I already knew that the term mouthpiece meant lawyer. The thing I was a little clouded on was just who was my lawyer?

A slender man in a black sports jacket stepped around Sandra and demanded, "Uncuff my client please!"

Withers, less than gently, undid the restraint around my wrist. He walked out of the interview room with Riley in tow. They looked ridiculous in those matching suits.

The lawyer sat in a chair opposite me. "I'm Sandra's cousin David," he announced handing me a business card. It read,

David Peel
ESQUIRE

Confusion etched lines into my forehead as I tried to put it all together. I asked Sandra, "How did you know I got hauled in?"

The door to the interview room opened slowly and there was Matthew Livingston. He held onto the door, preventing it from closing.

"I told her you were hauled in," he said confidently.

My body recoiled like a lash from a whip struck it. "How did you know I was here?" I accented the word 'you' heavily.

He stood solidly in the doorway still holding the door open. His head pointed downward for a second and then he slowly raised it. "Dennis, I don't understand why you insist on asking me questions that you already know the answers to."

A blank expression crossed my face. It must have been contagious because Sandra was wearing it also. The bench creaked as I leaned back against the wall and looked up at Livingston. "You thought I did this, didn't you?" My jaw muscles grew tight as I released the question.

Livingston's head pivoted, surveying the interview room. "If you insist on having this 'feel sorry for me' conversation can we have it outside? As your friend I advise you to not say another word."

"Why not," I asked still confused.

He pointed and said, "I'm not sure if it's obvious to you but it is to me. That cinderblock to the left of your head isn't made of concrete like the rest of the ones that make up this room. My guess is that it is concealing a recording device. Did they handcuff you right next to it?" My eyes widened as I observed the object that he spoke of. I hadn't noticed it the whole time I was there, but now it seemed clear as day. Running my finger against it I realized it was a cardboard square painted the same color as the rest of the concrete room.

"Let's get out of here," the lawyer said standing up. Sandra and I followed him. I turned to look at Matthew who was the last to leave closing the door behind him.

I lost track of time inside that interview room. When I stepped outside the night was black as ink and there was an added chill in the air. My guess was nine p.m. Sandra's watch said eight forty five.

I repeatedly thanked David Peel for coming to my rescue. I clasped his right hand firmly and shook it.

"Do you have any advice for me," I asked.

He looked at me for a second and replied, "Sure I do. You're a handsome young man; you should fix your hair a little bit better."

Touching my hair that refused to comply to the laws of style I decided I would let his little joke go unanswered. Kissing his cousin Sandra on the cheek he climbed into his car and took off.

I looked at Sandra and then at Matthew. I had been recently wondering if we were ever going to have another adventure like our last one. I never dreamed our reunion would involve bailing me out of a police station.

Matthew broke the silence that was clinging to the air. "Do you remember where Everest lives?'

I cocked my head and cast a thousand yard stare in his direction. "Of course I do, why?"

His return stare could have knocked me over. "Because we're going there now!"

"What," Sandra and I exclaimed.

CHAPTER 4.

I seriously could not believe what was about to take place. I had absolutely no shame about cowering in the back seat of Sandra's car as she turned onto Strand Street. Only ten minutes ago I was standing in the gravel driveway next to the police station thanking my lucky stars, and now my two friends were literally transporting me back to the scene of a crime that I was suspected of being involved in.

"Keep driving," Matthew said to Sandra as we approached the home of the now late Malcom Everest.

Butterflies were having a field day in my stomach as I decided to shut my eyes and black out these fears that were rapidly consuming me. I had no idea why Matthew wanted to go to the Everest home. If any of us were spotted around it the police wouldn't hesitate to haul me in again.

Peering out the back window, I noticed Sandra drove clear past the house. Perhaps they were just jerking me around about the whole affair. I exhaled and it sounded like someone punctured a car tire.

"So, you're breaking my chops Livingston?"

His knuckles were flattened against the passenger side window. Very tediously they began to rap out a rhythm against the glass.

"I want nothing to do with your chops, Dennis. I'm merely casing out the Everest estate."

My knees rose to meet my stomach and I felt what little warmth there was in my face dissolve.

"Casing out the estate, why?"

Sandra made a right turn, squaring the block. Matthew fixed a gaze upward. "When I feel you need to know that information Dennis, I'll…"

"Yeah, yeah," I flat out interrupted him, "I know, you'll be sure to let me know."

"Stop at the corner Sandra," Matthew said leaning forward to unzip something. From the backseat I guessed it was a knapsack. He yanked out a black overcoat and wrestled his arms into it. "If I'm not back in fifteen minutes, leave!"

Stepping out of the car he pulled a black hood that was attached to the coat over his head. His tall slender frame, now draped in black vanished into the darkness of the evening.

Sandra peered over her bucket seats at my cowering frame. I thought she was going to laugh.

"What," I demanded.

"Oh," she replied, "I was just wondering if the police conducted a cavity search?" Her comments were accompanied by a laugh that disrupted the quiet evening.

I wiped my wet palms against my knees and partially cracked a smile. "Real funny Sandra. Would you mind telling me what we're doing here?"

Sandra jerked back around to face the windshield. Her eyes volleyed back and forth between the windshield and the rearview mirror.

"I'm not sure but kid genius was hot to get over here, and fast."

"Why," I cried out. I felt robbed of any feeling of freedom by being dragged back here.

Sandra's red hair was dangling from underneath a black knit cap. Still examining the rearview mirror she sounded borderline parental when she addressed me. "You know Dennis, did it ever occur to you that your friend Matt might be trying to help you?"

I wiped my palms again. "You're right Sandra, and thank you for bringing your cousin today. I don't mean to come across ungrateful but I'm a little…scared."

A somber silence fell upon the interior of Sandra's car. Maybe she didn't know what to say. She continued to look at the rearview mirror, probably making sure no one was spying us.

"Here he comes," she announced.

The passenger door opened and Matthew slid into the seat.

"To the loft," he said.

Sandra dropped the car into drive and we were off. I waited a few minutes before I sat up in the back seat. Matthew removed the hood.

We got to Livingston's garage a lot faster that my feet carried me earlier that afternoon. Matthew hung the overcoat up after removing two plastic ziplock bags from an interior pocket. I tried to make out what was inside each of them. I had no idea. Matthew's eyes were locked on the bags. Whatever he was up to he seemed to be completely driven by determination.

Paranoia was like an insect creeping across me, I spoke up. "You know if you removed evidence from a crime scene, the police will probably make a bee line for my front door."

"Probably not," he said taking out a microscope. "I climbed through that narrow little window in the back room. It was pretty narrow, that should give you a rock solid alibi."

"Very funny," I replied, completely deflated. "Would you mind explaining what it is you're doing?"

He had a can of compressed air and was blowing it on the microscope lens. "They discuss things pretty openly on the second floor of the police station house. You'd be surprised just how openly. Now I'm curious Dennis, real curious!"

My hands danced between my knees, coat pocket, and my uncontrollable hair. I decided to sit on them. "Um..do you have any idea how hot a hot seat I'm sitting in over this matter?"

He placed the microscope and can on the wheel top and shot a glance in my direction. "You're the one always complaining about the lame stories they give you to cover for the Serling High newspaper. The way I see it you've just landed an investigative story here."

"What," I asked in a serious state of confusion.

"The school told you to write a story on Malcom Everest. So now you're going to report about the mysterious circumstances surrounding his death."

The corners of my mouth began to rise on their own. I announced it quietly, Dennis Sommers, Investigative Reporter. It had a real nice ring to it. Sandra began to jokingly brush off my denim as if I were royalty. Then, like a car crash in my head, I was shocked back to reality.

"But I don't know the circumstances surrounding Everest's death."

One of his eyes was glued to the microscope lens. He released it and looked sternly at me. "Can you give me a chance here, I'm working on it."

I calmed my hands that were fidgeting slightly, and said, "Sorry."

"Okay," he announced standing up. His usually neat clothes fell right into place as he stood straight as an arrow. He pointed in the direction of Sandra and me. "Meet me tomorrow before first period, the back entrance of the school. I need the two of you to bring a copy of every newspaper you can. I need to see if and how this story will be reported."

He sat back down and peered into the microscope lens again. "Now what I would like to do is in fact what I like to do, test a theory. May I have my small piece of happiness?"

It freaked me a bit at just what classified as happiness to Mr. Livingston.

"You must go now," he instructed us.

We did just that.

CHAPTER 5.

SILENCE IS GOLDEN

I got up earlier than usual the next morning. I needed to fill my parents in on just what happened last night. I grabbed them before they left for work. I told them everything from when I received my journalism assignment to when we left the police station. I did not get into Matthew's extracurricular activities at the Everest estate. I wasn't sure what he was fishing for but if it scared me it would mortify my folks.

Mom and Dad were extremely concerned, but as usual were satisfied that I handled myself maturely and did nothing wrong. They understood my interest in journalism and inspired it. I gave my father the lawyer's business card and he told me he would call Mr. Peel when he got to work. All was cool….for now.

Sandra was the best. She figured me to be a little stressed after the evening we experienced so she picked me up for school that morning. I felt a slight relief when I saw the familiar red Ford Mustang pull up in front of my house. We stopped at a newsstand and bought four newspapers.

We were early. Sandra parked by the rear of the school. We had a half hour before first period. I tilted my head to the right to take in the view of the back of the building. The emerald lawn descended in the direction of the rear door to the school. It was divided by a beige concrete path that ended at the maroon colored door. Behind that door was the hallway where the art department could be found. It was quite fitting; I thought to myself, Matthew Livingston looked like artwork himself emerging from that very door. His tan jacket was sculpted to his shoulder blades and on top of those shoulders was a head that seemed to hold endless amounts of fascinating facts.

He approached the car as Sandra and I got out. I clutched the newspapers under my right arm.

Matthew extended his left hand and I placed the papers in it.

"Fifth period," he sounded serious, "meet me in the auditorium. Do not discuss yesterday's events with anyone!"

"But what if Mr. C from the school newspaper wants…"

"NO ONE!"

His voice could have stopped my heart. It was like thunder disrupting a peaceful summer night. He cast a cold stare upon me. Then his voice calmed a bit.

"You can tell him after I've had a chance to look at these," he said holding up the newspapers. "Not before."

Placing the newspapers in his knapsack he walked toward the back door and I heard him mutter, "Silence is golden."

It was a grim thought he left us with, but it made sense. If he was on to something, secrecy was our best ally.

I must admit my mind wasn't on any of my subjects that morning. I still felt seriously violated by yesterday's events. From first through fourth period I literally spaced out on the green rectangular chalkboard in front of each classroom. My notebook was open and my pen was in hand, but I didn't write a word. This feeling I had was unshakeable.

Fourth period ended and I stepped into the auditorium. Matthew was seated in the front aisle with his eyes shut. Sandra, standing in front of him, rolled her eyes in my direction. Her shoulders went up about an inch and a half and then dropped. I assumed we were in for a strange occurrence with Mr. Livingston. My sneakers were sticking to the newly waxed auditorium floor. The wrenching noise they made as I pried them from the floor was enough of an indication to Matthew that I arrived. Like a window shade retracting sharply, his eyes appeared.

Staring at neither of us he announced, "Accidental death."

I exhaled in relief as if I actually got away with something. The corners of Sandra's mouth extended upward.

"Just one problem," Livingston continued.

I thought quietly, here we go again.

Matthew had placed his hands on top of his knees. His fingers got tense as they gripped the slacks he wore.

Looking up at me he said, "Malcom Everest was murdered!"

"What," Sandra and I exclaimed, simultaneously.

"The police have dismissed the matter as an explosion from the gas fireplace in the room. Four newspapers reported that very conclusion. I'm telling you he was murdered. Again, your silence is golden."

He rose from his seat and walked toward the exit. His pace was cool and calculated and it only added to the confusion that surrounded me. I found it amusing that his shoes didn't make any noise on the auditorium floor. I felt I needed to speak, so I spoke.

"And why does this concern us," I said toward his back.

He stopped walking and remained motionless for a moment and then turned quickly toward me. For a second I though I was going to get smacked. He stopped about three feet in front of me.

Keeping his voice low he said, "I believe when one human being murders another there are ramifications that affect many others. I have a feeling that is the case with Malcom Everest's murder."

My eyes blinked a few times and Sandra's scratched at the back of her head. I felt the need to ask something. So I asked, "What are the ramifications?"

No sooner did I ask I knew what he was going to tell me.

"When I feel you need to know that information, I will be more than forthcoming with it."

He left the auditorium.

CHAPTER 6.

Conversations With Sandra

Sandra Small worked part time at a cool little coffee shop called the Bean Counter. As I opened the door the aroma of fresh ground beans and hints of hazelnut washed over me. My eyes adjusted to the dim lighting that was situated around the walls which were painted a burnt orange. Café style tables and chairs were all around the room as customers sat reading newspapers, tapping away on lap tops, and working on crossword puzzles while drinking fresh coffee.

Sandra was behind the counter and when I took a seat at a vacant table she looked up. She raised her eyebrows to acknowledge me as she was counting money at an open register. Closing the register draw she said to the co-worker next to her, "I'm taking ten minutes."

She appeared at the table with a tray. Steam rose from two tall mugs sitting on top. Parking herself in a chair opposite me she placed one of the mugs in front of me.

"Thanks," I said taking a sip. She made it perfectly, half and half with no sugar.

"How are you feeling," she asked picking up a packet of brown sugar.

Placing my mug on the table I said, "A little odd."

She had the packet of sugar gripped tightly between two fingers of her right hand. Her left pointer finger was flicking away at it.

"Why's that?"

"Matt's freaking me out a bit. He seems bent on screwing with the police. And quite honestly, the idea of a murder scares me!"

Sandra was adding the sugar to her coffee.

"I understand how you feel Dennis. I've formed my own opinion of our rather strange friend. Care to hear it?"

"Shoot!"

She folded her hands and leaned in a bit. Steam from the mug danced across her face, slightly fogging the wire rimmed spectacles.

"Remember that night we broke up that cult at the old church. After it was all said and done, I was lying in bed that night. I couldn't sleep. Did you ever have that feeling that things happen for a reason?"

"No," I said refusing to accept reason in anything Matthew was doing.

She sipped the coffee and continued, "I think kid genius is special in some way. It's like he has an inner eye. He's capable where others aren't. I think that's because he cares to be capable. I think you and I inherited him for a reason. Like it or not the world has changed a lot in the last couple of years. I think we have an abundance of people who don't care to get involved even if getting involved is for a good reason. You ever hear the expression 'the largest journey begins with the smallest step'?"

"I guess I have."

"I think that journey is to make a change. We made a change in those peoples lives that night in the old church. We've got to take those steps. Give Matthew a chance! I guarantee something good becomes of it."

I finished my coffee and Sandra stood up.

"Maybe you should go visit him," she said.

Twenty minutes later I was entering the Livingston garage and making my climb to the loft. He was sitting on the edge of the old yellow sofa. On the wheel top was a microscope that he was perched over.

I didn't want to startle him like last time so I was relieved when he raised his left hand to acknowledge my presence. He continued to look through the microscope and then stood up.

"You still don't believe it was an accident," I asked.

Taking off his white coat he struggled for a second removing his right arm. With out looking at me he replied, "Everest's death was about as much an accident as would be my joining one of our school's social clubs."

Wow, I thought. He certainly was onto something. I proceeded with a new line of action. Taking a deep breath I bravely asked, "What can I do to help?"

He turned to face me and said, "I need a dentist!"

I studied him for a second. He didn't appear to be in any discomfort.

"A dentist," I asked, confused as usual.

His eyebrows scrambled closer together as his jaw tightened.

"Not just a dentist," he grinded out.

I snapped my fingers, trying to be quick in my guessing and said, "An orthodontist." I smiled, pleased with myself, thinking I had the right answer.

He stared at me as if I were from Mars.

"No, I don't need an orthodontist!"

I realized I should stop trying to guess Matthew's logic.

"Well then, what is it you exactly need?"

Quietly he asked, "Are you finished?"

I motioned my fingers across my mouth as if I were zipping it shut.

He sat on the sofa and rubbed his eyes.

"I need to find out who was Malcom Everest's dentist."

The hair on the back of my neck was at attention. Something was in the air and it was really creeping me out. I inhaled and felt my chest inflating slightly.

"I can do that," I said boldly.

"Good," he replied. "Now, do you own a sports coat?"

Oh yeah, the forecast called for confusion. I experience that a lot when I'm around Matthew.

"Why do I need a sports coat to find out who was Everest's dentist?"

"You don't," he said turning sharply toward the rear of the loft. "Sandra is picking you up tomorrow evening."

You know, I honestly found all of this amusing. The way everyone else planned my days was really amusing.

"And where is the lovely Ms. Small taking me?"

He sat on the couch again, methodically positioning himself to perch over the microscope.

"Springdale funeral home," he said adjusting a dial on the side of the device. When his eyes seemed to approve of what he was examining through the microscope lens, he looked up at me.

"Malcom Everest is being waked at 7 p.m."

I decided not to ask him the logic behind attending the wake of Malcom Everest. My face must have revealed just that.

"Sandra knows what to do. She'll fill you in at school tomorrow."

I nodded in agreement. I couldn't read what his mood exactly was. He was a cross between aggravated and confused. He quickly thrust his hand through the dark brown hair that hung close to his eyes.

I suddenly felt like I was disturbing the genius at work. The wood floor creaked beneath my heels as I turned to descend and leave.

"Dennis," he called and it echoed slightly in the loft.

My feet became motionless and my eyes peered over my shoulder. He remained seated.

"I need that information on the dentist tomorrow."

Realizing my evening was to be occupied with research and computer work I replied with zero enthusiasm, "You got it."

CHAPTER 7.

We Need A Dentist

The next morning after second period I was shoving some text books into my locker. When I looked up, to my displeasure, Derrick Porter was standing there. Mr. Super Senior, the self proclaimed know it all of Serling High was flanked by two other seniors who were standing sentinel like behind him. He needed that. The other two made Derrick look like a television character that had his own theme music.

"Sommers," he said with that arrogant chin ever present. "I hear you're such a great reporter that people are dying to be interviewed by you."

Right on cue, like a human laugh track, the other two began to cackle.

I was caught off guard so I didn't have a come back at the ready. It turned out I didn't need one. Sandra Small closed my locker door to get a clear view of Mr. Egomaniac. She put some oomph behind it clanging her bracelets against the door in the process.

"I'm sorry Derrick," she said with slivers of sarcasm decorating her voice. "Perhaps you haven't heard, Dennis has been promoted to the travel and tourism section of the newspaper."

She inched closer to him.

"In fact, this week he's going to be doing a story on that planet you come from."

Derrick backpedaled a bit, bumping into his buddies in the process.

She pressed on, "You know the one I'm talking about. The PLANET where everything revolves around YOUR shallow image!"

She stood fast and never broke eye contact. I fought the urge to laugh. Derrick Porter beat it down the hall with his lackeys right behind him.

I slid my combination lock into place and secured my locker.

"Nice job," I said smiling.

"Ick," she spat out the words in the direction Derrick had fled.

Tucking my binder under my arm, Sandra and I began to walk down the hall.

"Okay," she said, with much focus, as if the incident with Derrick Porter had never happened. "I'm picking you up tonight and we are attending the wake of Malcom Everest. It should be a sizeable turnout, so we shouldn't have a problem blending in. I figure I'll park across the street so we can see the front door. That way we can see when they have a pretty good crowd inside and make our entrance."

She handed me a sheet of paper and continued, "Everest is survived by two sisters. At some point we are going to express our condolences to them. On the sheet of paper you have there are some questions I need you to memorize. We have to slip them into our conversation. All we are doing is a bit of fishing for anything peculiar. We head to Matthew's afterward."

The bell rang and we broke off from each other. I headed to third period class.

When fourth period ended I strolled into the auditorium and Livingston was standing there doing anything but smiling. I handed him some papers that I printed out last night. His stare was penetrating me; I assumed he just wanted me to tell him what I came up with in my records check.

"Everest's dentist is Doctor Quinn. We have two dentists in town, I started my search there. My program that checks public records and billings indicates Everest saw Doctor Quinn, with the exception of two months last year. In that two month interim Doctor Quinn's patients were seen by Doctor Shaw. I seemed to recall the good dentist had a fire in his office so I checked on that and the dates coincided. Everything you want to know is in those printouts. The computer program in his office is so old I could hack into it in my sleep."

He seemed to drift off for a moment. In utter silence, he neatly folded into a seat in the front row.

"Doctor Albert Quinn," he said as if he were revisiting an old memory. "He grew up with my father. They were good friends."

"Sweet," I said as if a ray of optimism shined upon us. "Get your dad to call him up and you bounce whatever questions you have off of him."

He looked up at me for a second and then back down.

"You want to dig him up," he asked, "My dad has been dead for the last sixteen years."

At first I felt shock than I felt like a complete idiot. He didn't let me linger like that for long. His voice became somber for a moment.

"He died in the Gulf War when I was one year old. So I was told."

He tucked the papers into his binder and said, "My mother is still friendly with him. Perhaps I could ask her to help me with this one."

He walked out of the auditorium.

CHAPTER 8.

Drama at Springdale Funeral Home

At seven p.m. I sat shotgun in Sandra's car. I had dress pants on along with the sports jacket that I was practically under orders from Matt to wear. Yeah, I looked sharp! I tried a different approach with my hair for this occasion. I actually dried it with the gel already applied. Different story. Same ending. No spike.

Sandra got a perfect parking spot opposite the funeral home. We had a clear, unobstructed view of the front door. We were going to give it a half hour before we made our entrance. It only took about ten minutes before a sizeable crowd had entered. We decided to wait five more minutes and made our way.

I gazed down at the paper Sandra gave me. I felt prepared with the questions I was to ask Malcolm's sisters. I was a little nervous about this scheme. My palms were moist and the fluttering in my stomach felt like a bird was in there trying to get airborne.

The entrance to Springdale funeral home was meticulously maintained. Two older gentlemen in black suits opened tall glass doors for us to enter through. A light drizzle began to fall, so I wiped my feet on the fake grass doormat that was at the top of the stoop.

When we entered a dark silence consumed us. The carpet must have been vacuumed twenty times that day. It practically sparkled as we walked on it. An antiseptic feeling clung to the hallway as we turned to the viewing room for Malcom Everest. A strong odor of flowers was bullying my sense of smell. My stomach began its antics again. I saw elderly men and women, middle aged men and women, and even some youngsters. The place was jammed. My eyes leveled off on the dark clad individuals, rows of chairs uniformly placed, and finally the casket. The oak box was surrounded by flowers on top of flowers, but the most obvious thing wasn't obvious at all to me. The casket was closed!

I quickly removed my eyes from it. I was battling some sort of feeling of guilt, as if I were responsible for all of this. I had to remind myself that I wasn't. It had been a confusing way to start the week. Now I really wanted Matthew to figure this whole mystery out so I could at least straighten out my state of mind.

Glancing to my left I noticed Sandra. Her red hair was pinned up but some of it hung down on the side, slightly covering gold hoop earrings. Her black blouse sat perfectly in the long matching skirt, finished by black high heeled shoes. An older woman was grasping Sandra's right hand with both of hers.

"My condolences," Sandra said to the woman in a soft spoken voice that seemed to underscore the mood in the funeral home.

Looking around at all the people who came out to pay their respects, I suddenly felt bad at the way I referred to Malcom Everest when I first received my assignment. I believe there is an unfair prejudice against the elderly and I was guilty of it. Taking another glimpse of the room I realized a lot of these people must be big wigs in society. They probably ran in the same social circles as Malcom Everest.

Sandra took my hand and smiled.

"It's time," she whispered, leading me toward the casket. We were actually going to kneel in front of it.

As we did she continued to whisper, "The two sisters are sitting right behind us. The obituary listed their names as Dorothy and Lilith. I'm not sure who's who. Follow my lead anyhow."

The first rows of chairs were designated for immediate family. Having identified our targets, Sandra stepped in front of a salt and pepper haired woman. The woman glanced up at Sandra who smiled.

"Dorothy," she said bending down to the woman's level. It was a 50/50 chance on guessing which sister was which. It appeared that Sandra guessed right for the woman didn't correct her.

"I'm so sorry for the loss of your brother," Sandra continued.

"Thank you dear," Dorothy replied. She smiled through apparent sadness. There was a handkerchief grasped in her black gloved hand.

"This is my friend Dennis," Sandra said turning toward me.

It was show time! I tugged at the ends of my sports jacket and with an air of confidence I stepped forward and leaned in to offer my hand to the woman. She took it.

"So sorry for your loss," I said surprising myself with a touch of maturity. The grip underneath the dull material of her glove was slight. She made eye contact with me.

"I really admired your brother, he was a great man."

"Really," her lips parted to form a smile.

My nose twitched as the conglomeration of flowers made me want to sneeze. I ignored it and continued, "I've been studying business at school and Malcom was always kind enough to let me ask him some questions. He was a wealth of information and help to my studies."

The woman hesitated and I wondered briefly if she was on to me. Then she smiled and my stomach expanded in relief.

"So nice of you to be here," she said.

"Everyone must have loved your brother," I said glancing at the big turnout. I was just hoping for a groundball here. I wanted her to say something like everyone loved him except…

"Oh," she said, "I guess he was well liked."

"Of course he was well liked," another voice chimed in. It was another older woman dressed in black. Her hair had more salt than pepper to it. This had to be Lilith, Malcom's older sister. I glanced at her as she leaned into our conversation.

She continued, "Of course he liked our brother. Malcom always gave him those nice tips around the holidays. He deserved every one of them. Delivering the mail with such care and always helping with the big packages."

My face contorted into an expression that just cried out, 'WHAT?'

"Oh," Dorothy said with sudden enthusiasm, "I didn't recognize him out of uniform."

I needed to probe. I had to find out who Malcom Everest's close friends were and hopefully if he had any enemies. I was ready with my first question when Lilith said, "I think his uniform makes him look older." She was looking at her sister, but pointing at me.

"You know, you're right," Dorothy said nodding along with her sister.

"No, no, no," I said trying to clear their confusion, "I'm not the mailman, I'm Dennis Sommers. I'm…"

"Oh," Lilith gasped letting her gloved hand fall limp, "talk about those summers. It must be so hot carrying all that mail in such temperature."

Dorothy glanced at Lilith and then up at me, "It's a miracle you didn't get heat stroke, you know."

I felt as if a pin was stuck in my investigative balloon. These two were hopeless for getting information.

"Retiring soon are you," Lilith asked.

I felt useless. I turned to look at Sandra. Her head was bent slightly downward. She was sliding her hand horizontally in front of her neck in an effort to tell me to cut it off. I did.

She stepped closer to me and whispered, "I'll pull the car around."

I stood up straight and smiled at the ladies. Turning to leave, I heard one of them say, "He looks younger out of uniform." My guess was Dorothy.

Outside the funeral home the light rain that fell earlier had stopped, but dampness still clung to the air. A number of cars were parked and double parked in front so I turned and stood in the exit of the driveway.

It happened so fast. A flicking noise went off so close to my right ear it was startling. Before I could identify what it was a cold flat metal object was pressed against my throat. I felt someone behind me, probably the bearer of the knife. I couldn't turn to look or my throat would have been cut. All I could make out was a dark brown knife handle clamped in a large right hand. A gnarly right hand it was, the size of a brick, with a small tattoo in the shape of an anchor between the thumb and forefinger.

A male voice, definitely older, spoke, "This is the second time I've seen you kid. The first time was running out of a house on Strand Street, two days ago. I'm just making sure this is the last time …"

I don't know if he stopped speaking or I stopped hearing. My eyes were bulging as they got hit with a pair of headlights. I could make out Sandra's car heading straight for us. My heart beat began to run the forty yard dash.

The blade was released from my neck and I was shoved to the asphalt pavement. I rolled to my right away from the oncoming car. Screeching brake pads gripped tires that glided against the slick ground. I heard a commotion as my attacker was fleeing. I saw a dark suit and stylish shoes that clapped against the sidewalk as he ran. I got to my knees and started to cough. I had to pull it together for Sandra was out of the car with pursuit written all over her. She must have shed the high heels because she was barefoot; bolting down the block after the dark figure that disappeared down the street. She stopped and shouted to me, "Get in the car!"

It was one big blur to me as I climbed in the passenger's seat. The glowing dashboard light was creating one freaky atmosphere against the gloomy night. The car was still running as Sandra slid into the driver's seat, grasping the driver side door and slamming it behind her. She pivoted her head checking behind her while dropping the stick shift into reverse. There was a slight clunk as the transmission acknowledged. We sped backwards. Her right hand aggressively thrust the stick shift forward and the wheel spun for a second on the wet surface. My eyes were bouncing around my skull as Sandra floored it down the block. She hung a right turn that made her radials squeal. There was no one in sight. Sandra squared the block, but my attacker was gone.

I wasn't exactly sure what just took place, or why. I did know one thing; I knew where we were going. Determination was written across Sandra's face as she turned the car onto Baskerville Street.

CHAPTER 9.

My Dinner with Doctor Quinn

"Great," he shouted, springing up off the old yellow sofa. It was hardly the reaction I expected or, for that matter, wanted. After all I had just told him the whole story of me being threatened at knife point.

"What exactly do you find great about all of this," I exclaimed, staring at the grin on his face. It occurred to me that every time I got roughed up, he seemed happy.

"They've showed themselves." He gripped his chin and began to pace.

I think I understood what he was talking about, but the shock I suffered was still lingering. I felt like that blade was still against my neck.

Stopping in mid-pace he snapped his fingers and pointed at me. Can you tell me anything else about this man?"

"No, I can't."

"And the tattoo, you say it appeared to be an anchor?"

"Yes."

"Pointing up or down?"

I had to think for a minute as my life was passing before my eyes when I observed it. "Down," I said, reassuring myself.

"Hmmmm," he said gazing upward. "Australian."

Sandra called out, "How on Earth do you know that?"

"I've made a study of tattoo art and an anchor in that place and position is synonymous with Australian tattoo art. In fact the symbol is actually referred to as a hope anchor. Why people insist on wearing advertisements really perplexes me."

"You've been to Australia," she asked him.

"I've barely been out of this garage!" Pointing to me he said," You will be at my house at 7 p.m. tomorrow. We're having dinner with my mother and Doctor Quinn."

"Okay."

Sandra sat in a folding chair looking at the two of us and asked, "What do you make of all this?"

I figured the question was aimed at Livingston, so I listened while he answered.

"I think it's pretty obvious that someone recognizes Dennis. I think these actions are fueled by paranoia. Perhaps they fear Dennis observed something they didn't want observed. Honestly, someone wouldn't go to the extreme measures they went to tonight if Malcom Everest died from an explosion caused by his gas fireplace."

It made perfect sense. Someone had a guilty conscience, but whom?

"What did you learn from Everest's sisters," he asked me.

I looked at him and a smile constructed out of sarcasm crossed my face.

"Nothing my friend, I learned nothing. The two of them were so wacky that they thought I was their brother's mail carrier."

Sandra started to crack up.

"I'm thinking about telling them Malcom never tipped me for last years holidays."

Sandra was actually bent over in the folding chair, hysterical.

"You know," I began, far from amused, "you are the only people I know who find amusement in my misfortune."

Now they both lost it. The laughter was one huge cacophony that lasted for a solid minute. Matthew composed himself quicker than Sandra.

"Listen," he said with hints of amusement, "you can wear that sports jacket tomorrow, get some more use out of it."

Sandra was biting her lower lip. Her cheeks were expanded and looked like they were going to explode from laughter.

"Can we go now," I groaned.

She stood up, car keys in hand and said, "Sure."

"Sandra," Matthew spoke, "I understand you're working until eight tomorrow. Please come by after and join us for dessert."

"Thank you, I will," she replied.

"And Dennis," he added, "please bring your laptop. I suspect we might need it."

"Okay," I said nodding my head.

The next day at school was more of me attending classes with my mind glued on this little mystery that was unfolding. Who was the guy that grabbed me outside the funeral home? Why were they messing with me? Who and why did someone do in Malcom Everest, and should I abandon hair gel altogether and try mousse? My head remained in this fog until the school day ended.

At seven p.m., I was ringing the doorbell to the Livingston home. I had my sports jacket on and my laptop tucked under my left arm. I was about to run my right hand through my recently gelled hair. In fear of it getting stuck in there, I stopped. The door opened.

The slender woman with blond hair said, "Hello Dennis, nice to see you."

I had only met her once briefly, the first time I ever called on Matthew Livingston. That was before I knew my friend had a loft in his garage that he rarely left.

"Hi, Mrs. Livingston," I replied as she held the door open for me.

I entered the nicely decorated home. It reminded me of Matthew, the way he was well manicured. The dining room table was set and looked perfect. There was silverware, dishware, and candles…everywhere.

There was an upright piano against a wall in the living room with pictures and what appeared to be family heirlooms on top of it. I spotted a photo that had to be Matthew's father. I was inching closer to it for inspection when I heard my name called out.

Matthew had his arms folded across his chest. His black slacks matched his shirt that was buttoned up to his neck.

"Thanks for bringing the laptop," he said as the doorbell rang.

I could hear voices in the other room. I recognized Mrs. Livingston's; the other voice was male and older. Doctor Quinn.

Matthew walked into the dining room and I followed. He stopped, glancing at our dentist he whispered to me, "At least he came with one arm longer than the other."

I understood what he meant when I saw Doctor Quinn handing Mrs. Livingston a bottle of wine. His eyes perked up when he saw Matthew.

"Hello Matt," his jovial voice rang out. I guess I should consider myself lucky that I have a dentist who can be described as jovial.

They shook hands. Doctor Quinn was a nice man. He was a portly fellow with a round face and a forehead that kept going back. What little hair was on his head looked like it was hung out the window of a car that was doing about ninety miles an hour.

"I recognize you," he said lowering his eyebrows to a squint. "Smile," he said.

I felt like a jerk, but I quickly flashed a smile.

"Dennis Sommers," he said thrusting out his hand, I shook it. Honestly he only saw me three weeks ago so I know he was trying to put us on that he could tell my name by looking at my teeth. I guess it made him happy.

The three of us chatted for a few minutes and then we sat at the dining room table. I was checking out some of the food Mrs. Livingston began to serve. Matthew's eyes were pinned on the good dentist.

Doctor Quinn sure could talk. He sure could eat too. The cold antipasto, the hot antipasto, and forget about the lasagna. I couldn't count how many servings he had.

Matthew ate very little. All the food Mrs. Livingston prepared was delicious but Matthew was too busy studying Doctor Quinn.

Conversation was going on between the two adults and I heard Matthew's father mentioned a few times. Matthew looked like he was perched to interrupt them. He waited until they were finished talking.

"How's business Doctor?"

He took a sip of his wine and waved his hand in front of himself, "Great Matt. Thank you for asking."

Matthew lifted his fork to pierce a small piece of lasagna, but just grasped the utensil instead.

"Dennis and I are taking a class called *Introduction to Business management.*"

Doctor Quinn's eyebrows lifted half an inch indicating that he was impressed. For the record, myself and kid genius have never taken a class together.

"How does somebody," Matthew hesitated clutching his fork. "What I mean is how do you make a business decision in your profession. For instance your supplies, how do you decide who to order them from?"

Now it was Doctor Quinn who hesitated, slightly. "Well, uh," he sipped his wine again. "It's a combination of the reputation of a supplier and what is cost effective. Reputation is very important, but saving money is important as well. Remember Matt, never sacrifice quality to save money."

Matthew cocked his head to one side and asked, "Small supplies, like plastic cups and paper towels, how do you choose a vendor for those."

"There are many vendors for small items, so that is something you can totally base on cost efficiency."

"How about the big items?"

"Such as?"

Matthew's lips pushed out a bit as his head rocked from side to side. He seemed to be mulling over his answer and finally said, "Tools and machinery."

Doctor Quinn placed his palms flat on the table and said, "When it comes to tools and machinery you want top line items. If you shop around you might be able to save some money, but it's not likely to be much. Good equipment is in demand and the manufacturers know that."

Mrs. Livingston was smiling slightly. I think she found her son amusing and she certainly was giving him room to question Doctor Quinn.

Matthew leaned into the back of his chair and locked his hands in his lap. His chin lowered and his mouth rested even, not a smile or a frown. I wasn't sure what he was going to ask next. In the course of my youth Doctor Quinn removed a few of my teeth, but now it was the dentist who was having something extracted, namely information. There was tension underneath his smile. He took a big sip from his wine glass.

"You know I'm very interested in lab work," Matthew said motioning in the direction of the garage. I have a small set up myself. Who makes your dental implants?"

His eyes took in Matthew and me. Placing his glass down he said, "I use an excellent company."

"And what is the name of this excellent company?"

He smiled and looked around and then said, "Russo Manufacturers. They are renowned makers of false teeth and dental bridges."

"Wow," Matthew said, sounding impressed, "do they do all that on site?"

"That's the beauty of it. All work is done on site and since they are local, I always have my orders delivered on time, if not early. You see Matt, that's another deciding factor when choosing a company, location."

Matthew turned to me and asked, "Are you getting all this Dennis? We're going to ace this class, especially with all this first hand knowledge, thanks to Doctor Quinn."

He relaxed a little and smiled, "Glad I could help boys."

Mrs. Livingston asked if anyone wanted any more and Doctor Quinn declined politely. I did the same. I was pretty full where as Matthew ate next to nothing.

I stood to help Mrs. Livingston collect the dishes.

Doctor Quinn stood also and asked, "Would you excuse me for a minute." He removed a cigarette from a metal case. "Bad habit," he said shrugging his shoulders. He walked toward the side door. Matthew rose and followed him.

Mrs. Livingston took the collected dishes from my hands. "Go with him," she insisted. "Make sure he doesn't do anything strange."

I was about to supply a comeback to that statement, but swallowed it instead.

The side door led to the driveway that was in front of the garage. Three garbage cans were lined to the left. To the right, puffing away was Doctor Quinn. Approximately two feet in front of him stood Matthew Livingston.

The tension was so thick you could slice it. Doctor Quinn inhaled on his cigarette. The paper crackled as it burned. A gray cloud of smoke enveloped his head as he exhaled. Perspiration clung to his forehead.

Matthew looked him in the eyes as he commented, "The Russo family runs a lot of things in this town. Construction, sanitation, should I continue? Or should I break out my dictionary and we can look up the word criminal together."

Doctor Quinn inhaled viciously on his cigarette and coughed.

"Matt," he replied defensively, "I can see so much of your father in you. He was always looking beneath the surface of things. I assure you all is well."

"Sure," Matthew said, "so a year ago when I sat in another dentist's office, awaiting a filling, because you had a fire in your office, all was well then? Am I in the ballpark here?"

Another puff of cigarette smoke clouded the air. Matthew didn't give him a chance to say anything.

"I never knew my father, you did. As a favor to him could you please tell me?"

The dentist coughed again and finally spoke, "Yes, you are in the ballpark."

"Thank you," my friend replied, "let's have some coffee."

Doctor Quinn discarded his cigarette in one of the garbage cans and we went back inside.

CHAPTER 10.

DEVALUED

When we went back inside, Sandra was there happily getting acquainted with Mrs. Livingston. Matthew's mother turned to face us and said, "Sandra arrived while you boys were outside chatting. She was nice enough to bring us some fresh ground coffee. It's brewing right now."

"Thank you Sandra," Matthew was the first to say.

I was fixated on her for a moment. She certainly could illuminate a room. The spell was broken by Doctor Quinn who shook hands with her.

We all sat and there was a new set of dishes on the table. Coffee mugs replaced the dinner glasses. Mrs. Livingston placed a cake pedestal on the table and on top of it was a key lime cheesecake. It looked amazing.

Matthew tugged at my sleeve. I looked at him and he turned to take in Doctor Quinn who was talking with Sandra. Turning back to me he said, "After dessert, fire up your laptop. Find Russo Manufacturers and get directions there."

Mrs. Livingston appeared with the coffee pot and poured some for Doctor Quinn first. She then filled Sandra's cup followed by mine and then Matthew's. She then sliced the cheesecake and served everyone in the same order. Matthew didn't even lift his fork.

The next half hour was pleasant conversation that erased the mood that surrounded the table earlier. Everyone chatted pleasantly except Matthew who sipped his coffee while appearing deep in thought.

When Doctor Quinn said his goodnights I shook his hand and took the opportunity to tell another lie. I thanked him and told him I would let him know how I made out in that business management class I was taking.

Matthew walked him to the door and a few words were passed that I couldn't hear. From where I stood you would have thought Matt was the adult between the two of them. He seemed to be assuring the dentist that there were no hard feelings.

I was on my laptop using a search engine to pull up the address for Russo Manufacturers. I memorized the cross streets and shut down my computer.

Walking back into the dining room, laptop under my arm, Sandra and Mrs. Livingston were collecting the plates. Matthew was where I left him.

"Thank you Mother," he said.

"You're welcome Matt," she replied. Her eyebrows bent inward as she gazed at her son. "You look different. How are you feeling?"

He drew breath slightly and released it. "Devalued!"

Mrs. Livingston placed the dishes she was holding down on the table. "Your talk with Doctor Quinn wasn't what you expected?"

He appeared to be confused as he gazed upon his mother. I started to see a family resemblance and could almost picture what his father would look like if he were here today. Yet there was something that hadn't been added to my equation. Where did this restless intellect, which drove a seventeen year old to extremes, actually come from?

Matt turned away from his mother and sighed, "I guess my desire to understand human behavior leaves me feeling….devalued."

I guess she understood him. She was nodding her head as if she did.

I didn't understand, as usual.

CHAPTER 11.

EVIL IN THE NIGHT

Sandra was seated in the driver's seat, I sat shotgun, and Matt was centered in the back seat. Sandra had her keys in the ignition but hadn't started the car.

"Where are we headed," she asked, turning to face him.

"Dennis," his voice came from the backseat, "you have the directions to Russo's, don't you?"

"Yes," I answered not bothering to look in the back seat. "Why are we going there?"

"Reconnaissance!"

"What," Sandra and I spat out simultaneously.

"Reconnaissance," he said slowly. "The word is old world French, meaning recognition. It was adapted by the military for the purpose of gathering information by examining the ground of a location."

I wondered if Matthew shook his head hard enough, what might fall out. I told Sandra the cross streets and she started the car and drove off into the night.

We were ten minutes into town when the local streets and stop signs transformed into avenues and stop lights. The sight of houses became the sight of offices and the occasional fast food stops. The car rolled on as the closed and sometimes gated store fronts gave way to a few blocks of small factories. Cold lifeless exteriors occupied sections of the sidewalks, equipped with barred and sometimes bricked up windows. Sandra braked at a red light and I saw a white brick structure on the opposite side of the intersection. Over the front door in black letters it read

RUSSO MANUFACTURER

"That's it on the left," I announced.

"Square the block," Matthew said.

She drove slowly past the factory that loomed unlit on the corner. The car went around the block and when we were directly behind Russo's, Matthew asked her to park. All three of us got out. I was really curious about what Matthew was up to. At the rear of Russo's building was a small docking bay. A metal platform hung off the rear of the building and a large cargo van, unoccupied, was backed up to it. I assumed it was there for loading in the morning. Matt stared feverishly at it from the side walk.

"Big van," he said examining the long vehicle. Pointing at it he asked me, "Do this many people have bad teeth?"

Okay, I could see why he was curious. I wondered myself as I looked around. The night time atmosphere in the business district was silent and somewhat sterile. An occasional car would hiss down the main avenue, but they were few and far between. Matthew continued to take in the cargo van, which was labeled for deliveries, when the three of us suddenly spun around.

The throttling vibration of a motorcycle filled the night. At first it sounded as if it were right behind us, but no. It was on the main avenue.

A revving noise rang out in the night like a siren, and then stopped. Whoever was riding was on the other side of Russo's.

Sandra said, "I'm taking a peek."

Her legs were in slow motion, stepping lightly around the corner of the building. Her arms were still and her frame hung close to the side of the building as she went.

I felt tired as my back sunk against the white brick wall. Matthew was wide eyed and attentive. Perhaps my full stomach was causing my fatigue. I placed my hands in the pockets of my sports jacket. A slight chill invaded our space. My eyes were closing when I caught a glimpse of Sandra returning.

"Okay," she said. "There's a biker-looking dude out front. He's wearing a denim jacket with the sleeves cut off. On the back is a big painted skull with a flaming sword going through the center of it."

I looked right at her and said with no hesitation, "Savage Sword Skulls!"

It was a gang that rode on motor cycles and fought with anyone who threatened their patch of concrete, the parking lot in the upper level of Down River Park. They were older than us by a few years, but a lot of people in Serling High knew them by reputation.

"That's not all," she added, "someone's in this building and they let the guy in."

Matthew turned to face us and asked, "Weren't Savage Sword Skulls in the newspaper recently?"

I remembered exactly what he was talking about. "Yes, someone did a drive-by shooting and one of their members got clipped."

Snapping his fingers and pointing in my direction Matthew said excitedly, "Exactly, and no one could identify the shooter."

"Rumor has it that it was the Urban Kings. They are the other gang, no motorcycles, yet. The bikes are supposed to be on order."

Sandra let out a quick laugh.

I asked Matthew, "What do you think this guy is doing here?"

He looked sharply at me and I said, "Yeah I forgot, when you think I need to know, you'll tell me."

"At least we'll know when he leaves since he drove in on such a loud apparatus. I'll never understand why people insist on hanging such advertisements on themselves."

I realized what Matthew meant. The loud motorcycles, the painted jacket, it was one big advertisement. If this guy was up to something he wasn't being that discreet about it. I guess that was to our advantage.

We had to wait it out in the rear of the building. If we walked around to the front we would be spotted easily, especially at this hour.

Matthew was squatting like a baseball catcher. He had his head cocked to one side and his eyes shut. A minute later he opened them as a distant cranking noise was heard. Shortly after the cranking came the loud wailing of the motorcycle engine. It roared through the night and then disappeared.

"Do you want to tell me what a member of the Savage Sword Skulls is doing at Russo's Manufacturer's after hours," he asked me, still squatting.

My hands found their way into my coat pocket and my shoulders lifted an inch and dropped. I had no clue.

"I know," Matthew said seriously. "But I want more information." Thrusting a finger at me he said, "And you're going to retrieve it for me."

"And where shall I do said retrieving?"

"Why don't you start over there," he said pointing to an alley way that ran between two buildings in the middle of the main street.

I took a few steps in that direction and noticed a homeless man sitting at the edge of the alley way.

"Okay," I said boldly, "I'll ask him."

I started to walk toward the man and I was yanked back by Matthew who had my jacket collar. He slapped a five dollar bill into my hand and said, "Now ask him!"

I walked to the other side of the street and looked upon the man who was sitting with his back against the wall of the building. Litter was spewed around the alley way. Clutched in the right hand of this individual was a dark green bottle with a brown paper bag wrapped around it.

I looked at his face that was gazing at nothing. It told the tale of a hard life and he wore it like a road map.

On top of that face was hair like strands of steel hanging disorderly.

I wasn't sure if I should squat down or remain standing. I decided to meet my indecision in the middle and got down on one knee. I had the five dollar bill folded in my right hand so it appeared visible. Something about this man told me his reversal of fortune, for the worst, had been recent. His eyes glanced at the money for a second and then upward. He wasn't about to beg for it nor did I want him to. I wanted to know about our motorcycle visitor and this guy looked like he occupied this alley way quite frequently. Perhaps he could shed some light on all of this.

I extended the money toward him and he took it.

"Are they always open this late," I asked jerking my thumb in the direction of Russo's.

His overgrown eyebrows moved a little as he gazed past me. "Nah, not always."

His somewhat steady hand, that was darker than his complexion, lifted the bottle to his lips and he drank.

I noticed his fingernails were also dark and in bad need of trimming.

"They closed at six today. Someone came back about an hour ago and went inside."

"The motorcycle," I asked, "seen him before?"

"Twice before. Can't miss him when he comes around. Disturbs what little peace I get over here."

I thought for a moment before asking the next question. "Do you know either of them?"

He waited a moment before telling me no, but added, "The guy inside drives that pick-up truck." He pointed down the block to a dark blue truck that was parked opposite Russo's.

After thanking him I returned to my friends. I gave them the details of our conversation. The whole picture was becoming clearer now. Matt was not keen on this manufacturer, going back to our conversation with Doctor Quinn. Now a member of a gang was meeting one of their employees after hours.

"Let's get out of here," Matthew suggested.

Sandra took her car keys out of her pocket and an idea popped into my head.

"Drive past the pick-up truck," I asked her, "I want to get the license plate number."

She nodded her head approvingly. We had resumed our same seats in the car. As she cruised slowly past the vehicle, I took out my reporter's notebook expecting to jot down a bunch of numbers when I noticed there weren't any, just letters. It was a vanity plate that spelled, 'Russo Jr.'

Matthew looked at the plate and asked, "Why do people insist on advertising?"

We spent very little time in Matthew's loft that night. It was getting late and the three of us needed to digest some information. Beginning with our dinner with Doctor Quinn to our surveillance of Russo's, it was a long night.

Matthew sat on the yellow sofa, his forefingers massaged his temples. As usual he looked at neither Sandra nor me.

"These territorial disputes, these gangs, do you know much about them?"

His question was aimed at me. "Sure, I hear things at school."

He leaned back on the sofa and looked across the wheel top where Sandra and I were sitting on folding chairs.

"I fear something terrible is about to transpire. I need the two of you to find out where."

Sandra, who was sitting backwards on the folding chair, stood up.

"Tomorrow is Friday. Rave parties and other knuckleheaded functions take place on Friday's."

Looking at me he asked, "What was that gang that was suspected in the drive-by shooting?"

"Urban Kings," I replied, sure of myself.

He sat up. "They could very well be the targets of serious violence. Find out if they are planning something, and where."

Sandra patted me on the arm and said, "I'll pick you up early tomorrow. I have an idea."

Matthew looked at me and then at Sandra. "Go now. You need rest and I have more work to do."

I stood up next to Sandra and asked him, "When are you planning on getting some rest?"

He stood also and said, "If someone else dies over this whole mess we're looking into, I'll find it very hard to rest."

My back stiffened up as I realized the impact of his words. They were chilling. I looked at Sandra, she at me and we split.

CHAPTER 12.

FRIDAY MORNING FISHING

Friday! Sandra parked at the rear of the school and we walked to the front of the building. She pointed across the street and said, "There's our source of information."

Now check this out. I'll never understand this one. Across the street from Serling High School are a row of garden apartments. They literally face the front of the school. A group of students gather there every morning. Looking at my watch I noted that not only do they gather there, but they even show up early to do it. Each garden apartment has a concrete stoop in front of it and these students find one set of steps to sit on, all day. At least until the truancy officer showed up. Honestly, about fifty yards away is the front door to an education. I guess that was why we were going to ask them where a neighborhood gang was going to throw a party.

It was twenty five minutes before first period when Sandra and I crossed the street. There was only a hand full of guys hanging out, but there would be more on the way shortly. In about ten minutes the area would be a wall of cigarette smoke and foul language. Sandra headed straight for one guy who was distanced a bit from the others. I had seen him before but didn't know his name. He was laying back on the top step staring into the swaying green of the trees above.

"Hey," Sandra said waving her hand about six inches in front of his face. He didn't even acknowledge it. It was eight o'clock in the morning and this guy was baked. Not exactly the picture of health. Oh well.

"Huh," was his reaction still staring at the tree tops.

"Big bash tonight," Sandra bluffed, "heard about it?"

In his trance he somehow reacted defensively, "Course I heard 'bout it."

"Yeah right," she chuckled, "you lie."

"Roosevelt Park, lower level parking lot, Urban Kings."

She turned to me and said, "Our work here is done."

We crossed the street and headed into school. I told Sandra I would try to confirm the details being that our source of information was mentally visiting another planet. We headed to our first period classes.

Fourth period let out. I headed to the auditorium. Matthew Livingston was seated in the auditorium. He was an enigma to say the least. I doubt he slept much last night yet you couldn't find a wrinkle on him.

Sandra entered and asked, "Did you confirm it?"

"Yes, two other people gave me the same information as the human vegetable."

She looked down at the seated genius and said, "Roosevelt Park, lower level parking lot, some time this evening."

"I'm hearing after eight," I added. "The park closes at seven."

Matthew looked up at us and asked, "What goes on at one of these functions?"

I turned to Sandra to see which one of us was going to tackle the question and it was her. "The Urban Kings are there. Someone's car will be pimped out with a bass driven sound system. Crates of booze will be in abundance while lots of people with no significance in their lives will praise these losers."

His head went side to side in disbelief. "Okay," he began, "do not go into Roosevelt Park. Spy the parking lot from the perimeter. You should have an adequate view from several points. If our motorcycle friend from last night shows up, split! It could be a very dangerous situation."

"You expect an incident," Sandra asked.

"Based on what transpired last night I do."

I didn't quite follow him so I asked, "Something happen when I went to talk to that man last night?"

His forehead showed signs of creasing and his eyes were beaming right at me. "No, something happened when you were standing next to me."

I looked at Sandra and her at me. Clueless!

He continued with instructions, "On the north west corner of Union Street is an artifact called a payphone. If some sort of catastrophe takes place, go to it and dial 911.

Do not use your cell phone! I want no traces, especially not with Dennis' popularity lately with the police."

He stood.

"What are you going to do while Sandra and I are looking into this?"

He had started to walk out of the auditorium and said, "I'm going to figure out who killed Malcom Everest."

"And what does one have to do with the other?"

I'll chalk it up to him possibly being tired that I didn't get slapped. He just walked up to me and said softly, "It's all relevant."

Wow, I thought while watching him depart, his brain was firing on all cylinders.

CHAPTER 13.

Fireworks and Chaos

Sandra finished work at seven o'clock and picked me up at seven-thirty. My eyes went large when I climbed into the passenger seat. She was wearing a leather jacket with the sleeves cut off. Underneath that was a tattered denim jacket. A short brimmed cap was on her head backwards. The best way to describe her whole image was…defiant!

"Lose your denim," she said, "I've got something for you."

She pointed into the back seat and there was a battered looking leather bomber jacket. The black had worn its way white in many places and crease had become cracks in various parts of the material. It was still cool. I put it on. It was a size too big, but rebellion consumed me the second I flipped the collar up.

"Now this is bad," I called out as nervousness and excitement clashed in my stomach. "I may just crash the Urban King's party tonight."

"No you won't," she said stepping on the accelerator and knocking me back into my seat. "Matthew gave us instructions for a reason."

"Yeah, yeah," I groaned. My curiosity was piqued and for once I wanted to know what one of these parties was like.

It was just after eight when Sandra cruised past Roosevelt Park. We just wanted a glimpse of what was going on. There was a gathering in the parking lot.

I could feel the vibration of music. A car in the center of the lot had its hatch back open and two large speakers were literally erupting. Three metal garbage cans had orange flames dancing above their rims. It seemed as if the Urban Kings liked to have bonfires for their rituals. Spread around the lot were gang members, girls, and groupies.

Sandra ditched the car a few blocks away. There wasn't anywhere outside of the parking lot to leave it without being noticed. We crossed Union Street and hit the actual corner of Roosevelt Park. The party was happening about two hundred feet away. The music sounded a lot closer.

She put her arm out to block me although my feet wanted to keep on walking. I guess I really was curious.

I stopped and was still having a hard time remembering that it was actually Sandra in the whole get up.

"No further," she said sharply.

"I can go in there," I argued tugging on my mean looking leather.

"And do what, get killed?"

She certainly got right to the point. I didn't know any of these people and walking into this event uninvited might cause some problems, namely for me.

Well if I wasn't at the party the best thing I could do was observe it. I needed to get better at that anyway. Matthew Livingston observes everything.

Let me see, where shall I start? There was only one driving entrance into the lot. At the rear, where concrete met the expanse of the green grass was about nine parked cars. The one with the sound system was smack in the middle. The stench of burning wood and whatever else was in those cans drifted into the night. Tall guys with shaved heads and goatees were guzzling cans of something, probably beer. Their leather jackets and leather vests clung tightly, especially in the middle where a few of them had sizeable guts protruding. They didn't look like the cleanest bunch of guys either.

My observation exercise didn't last much longer. I heard the interruption and Sandra's eyes perked up from underneath her cap. Even with the blaring of the music I heard the rumbling of motorcycles. I didn't see any yet, nor could I determine the direction they were coming from.

"Here we go," Sandra said with a hint of despair.

I turned and looked in the direction of the North West corner to check for the payphone Matthew said was there. It stood about two feet in from the curb. As I examined it the noise grew louder and they appeared. I lost count after the eighth bike rounded the corner. Low profile motorcycles clung close to the ground as they went into their turn. I could see the painted jackets; it was the Savage Sword Skulls. Long silver exhaust pipes shot down the length of their vehicles and kicked up small clouds of gray exhaust.

The head rider was clutching something in his raised right hand as the line of bikes stormed into the parking lot. The object was white and cylindrically shaped. From the light of the burning garbage cans I could see him stop and launch the object in the direction of the car that was cranking out the music.

I don't recall what was going through my mind when a sheet of blinding white flashed across the parking lot. A second later a deafening boom echoed throughout the night.

I fell backward partially on Sandra. My face hit the cold grass as ringing filled my ears. A phantom force was pinning me earthward. I looked up and it was raining broken glass over the parking lot. The music was gone and the center car was in flames. One of the burning garbage cans had landed on top of it.

About three Urban Kings got to their feet and grabbed the head biker who was also down from the impact. A flurry of fists pounded him where he laid. It erupted, carnage, pure carnage. The two rival gangs were entangled in the center of the parking lot. It started to spread. Two guys from the Savage Sword Skulls were on their bikes trying to retreat. One was getting pummeled across the back by an Urban King armed with a long flaming piece of wood, which spilled out of the metal can. The biker fell to the ground while his buddy managed to get his motorcycle situated and took off in the direction he was facing, right at us! The bike went onto the grass when we noticed the piece of lumber, still on fire, soaring in the air like a javelin, thrown by his assailant. It landed in the rear rim of the fleeing motorcycle. The bike buckled and the rear wheel lifted high in the air sending its rider airborne. His arms and legs were swimming in the sky. A heavy set guy he was, and he landed with a thud that shook the ground. Actually it was more like a splat. He was on his back, motionless. His helmet had bounced off his head and rolled close to me.

Now came the scary part, the motorcycle was also airborne. It was spiraling through the air lit by the glow of the flaming lumber protruding from the rear wheel. It landed about ten feet away from us and the flickering torch-like stick bounced loose onto a small hill behind us. Sandra turned and looked in that direction and I heard a whooshing sound. There was a tall row of dry brush on top of the hill. It was now a wall of fire stretching to the sky.

The fighting had grown. Bodies were racing in our direction where the brawl had literally spilled.

Sandra sprang to life. The biker who crash landed was down and out and Sandra picked up his helmet and thrust it into my hands.

"Put it on!"

I could hear her order clear above the mayhem. My hands were shaking at the thought of what she might have in mind. I lowered my head to jam the helmet on. When I looked up Sandra was picking up the motorcycle that was still running. She leapt onto the seat and revved it up, causing the back wheel to kick rightwards in the process.

"Get on!"

I did just that as the chaos continued. I wasn't really thrilled with our options for escape. We were in the middle. On one side there were two rival gangs pounding the living daylights out of each other. On the other side was a hill with an impetuous inferno at the top of it.

The motorcycle was a radically aerodynamic looking beast, and Sandra fed it gas. The bike responded with heart pounding acceleration. I clung on for my life.

She nailed it and the bike responded. I looked down at the narrow frame we were sitting on and thought a better name for this vehicle would be a 'coffin for two'. I had no choice in the matter; she was flying towards the fiery ascent. She revved it hard and I could feel the tires fight the resistance of the incline. It climbed, we climbed. The tone of the engine hit an immensely high pitch and the next thing I knew we were soaring above the flames. Perspiration raked across my face as the fire was brushing the wheels beneath us. We just cleared it.

NOW WE HAD TO LAND!

Our soaring was much faster on the way down, obviously. My stomach felt hollow and my legs went numb. The motorcycle hit the ground and the suspension revolted on impact. I've no idea how she pulled it off, but we escaped.

I could see the pay phone on the corner and I became aware that we never called 911 but I don't think it mattered. Sirens were wailing in the distance. Sandra stopped the bike by the payphone and laid it down after we got off. I dropped the helmet next to it and we ran in the direction of where she left the car.

Once we were safely inside I thought about what just happened. I couldn't believe what we just experienced. The sirens got louder. I could tell Sandra's adrenaline was pumping because she started the car and tore off quickly. About ten minutes later we were parked in front of the Livingston house. We headed for the garage.

CHAPTER 14.

SHOELESS AND CLUELESS

"Exactly what I expected," Matthew said seated on the yellow sofa with the microscope still on the wooden wheel top in front of him. Sandra and I had just filled him in on the evening's festivities.

"How did you know?" I asked in a voice that was somewhat unstable. "And where did you learn to ride a motorcycle," I fired the last question at Sandra who was sitting on the folding chair backwards.

Matthew and Sandra looked at each other and she answered first, "You build it, I'll ride it."

Matthew looked at me and replied, "When I feel you need to know that information I'll be efficient in providing it. For now, I did some poking around. The car we saw outside the manufacturer belongs to Martin Russo Jr. He was arrested a few times when he was younger but never did any jail time. Now he runs one of the many family businesses, namely Russo's Manufacturers."

He handed me a piece of paper with an address written on it.

"You're going there tomorrow."

"To see who," I asked.

He smiled and said, "Malcom Everest's sisters."

"No," I said quite vocally.

"Yes," he said calmly.

"Why?"

"You're going to find out who Malcom Everest knew that spent time in Australia."

Sandra and I looked at each other. I remembered the incident at the funeral home and the tattoo on the man's hand.

"You really think..."

"Not only do I think it was him, I believe he was in the house before you got there. You said the front door was slightly open, probably because this person left in a hurry."

It was a bit creepy thinking back to the whole scene and realizing that I could have possibly brushed paths with this killer. Unknowingly, I began to pace.

Matthew broke the moment of silence, "Listen up. Since today is Friday, the last business day of the week, I believe more of the explosives you saw tonight are going to be moved tomorrow."

"Tomorrow," Sandra asked.

"Yes, Saturday is a perfect night to do it. No business is being conducted; the town will literally be vacant. In the evening the dark will offer even more concealment. If they are using that cargo van we saw the other night, they have all of Sunday to return it for Monday morning without arousing suspicion."

I felt the urge to scratch my head, but remembered the hardened gel that had been squashed by a motorcycle helmet. It actually made my hair look like a helmet, and a bad one.

"Why do you think they are going to move this stuff?"

He didn't look at me but answered, "If the police haul in one of these Savage Sword Skull members they might find out where the explosive was obtained. That would threaten exposure of this evil business that is being conducted."

"Hard headed those Skulls are," Sandra said, "pun intended. They'll deny having any possession of that explosive."

"I agree with her," I said.

"Still," he insisted, "rumors travel fast. They'll have to get rid of this stuff fast, before the police start looking for it."

"I'm home from work around five-thirty tomorrow," she said. "What time do you want to roll?"

"Whoa," I called out, "where are we rolling to? You don't mean to suggest that we are going to intercept a shipment of explosives? Here," I said taking out my cell phone and extending it toward Matthew. "Dial 911, it's on me."

He looked down and then up and then at me. "Do you really want to get reacquainted with the police? I'm not saying I'm positive about this shipment, but it seems likely to me."

I slapped my right hand against my forehead and the noise underscored my disbelief at what I was hearing.

"What's the matter," he asked.

"Oh nothing," I replied with much sarcasm as I began my pacing again. "It's just that I've been roughed up a few times this week, then sister daredevil over here rode a motorcycle with me on it and jumped Mount Incandescent."

Sandra shook her head saying, "It wasn't that big."

"Now we're going to stop a truck full of explosives."

"Precisely," he said.

"Oh no," I groaned.

"Are you finished?"

"For now."

"Find out everything you can from the sisters. It sounds like they really took a shine to you so it should be no problem."

"Matt," I partially shouted, "they're nuts!"

"Oh will you give it a shot. You'd be surprised at what older people can remember."

Sandra stood up and asked, "So I'll meet you here around seven?"

"That will be fine," Matthew replied.

"Anything else," I asked before turning to leave. "Could you possibly ask me for anything else?"

He stood up, looked at me and started to inspect my clothing.

"Yes," he said.

I looked at Sandra and she appeared to be in the dark on this one, so I asked, "What?"

"Give me your sneakers."

I refused to even argue and just kicked them off my feet. He picked them up and walked to the rear of the loft.

Since I was shoeless, I was really grateful to Sandra for the ride home she gave me.

CHAPTER 15.

I'VE NEVER BEEN TO AUSTRALIA

It was around noon the next day when I put on my sports jacket and after a quick stop at the post office, walked about a half a mile to 12 Mandelbaum Lane, where Lilith and Dorothy Everest lived together. Matthew must have been right about the impression I left on the sisters because they remembered me right away. They still thought I was their brother's mailman. Exactly how they were acquainted with their brother's mail carrier…you know something, I didn't want to know. Their confusion in this matter wasn't a bad thing; I could use it to aid in my investigation.

I had my excuse for visiting all planned out. I reached into the pocket of my sports jacket and removed the change of address forms that I grabbed from the post office.

"These are for you," I said extending a couple of copies of the form toward Dorothy. "You may want to forward your brother's mail here so you don't have to make the trip over to his house to collect it."

"Thank you," she said.

Lilith added, "Malcolm always said you were thoughtful."

"Yes," Dorothy agreed with her, "you're very thoughtful. Sit down and have some tea with us."

I sat in a sofa chair and the ladies sat on the couch opposite me. In between us was a steaming pot of tea and three cups. Now the tea pot was sitting in what appeared to be a knitted sweater, multicolored.

"That's a tea cozy," Dorothy said after she poured me a cup. "It keeps the pot warm."

She must have seen my eyes gazing at it peculiarly. This was nice. Today I learned what a tea cozy is and tonight Matthew Livingston was going to drag me along to stop some maniac who is exporting plastic explosives. It was quite the life for a sixteen year old. Anyhow I needed to complete this mission Matthew sent me on. I got right to the point.

"Did your brother ever go to Australia?"

The sisters looked at each other, tea cups in hands, and Lilith replied, "Malcolm's best friend Daniel Barton lived in Australia, Malcolm visited him a few times."

Home run, I thought to myself.

Dorothy lowered her head and said softly, "He passed away five years ago."

Strikeout, I thought to myself.

Dorothy, looking at my dejected expression said, "Malcolm took good care of his son Ensley. He guided Ensley in starting his own business here in the States."

Hope.

I smiled and asked, "How old is Ensley?"

Again the sisters silently conferred with each other and Lilith replied, "I believe he is in his early forties."

The memory raced through my head of that scene outside the funeral home. I remembered the knife at my throat, the threats, and the scare I got. A chill raced up my spine. Suddenly I was taking the whole thing personally. I wanted Livingston to unravel whatever was going on and nail this guy. If it was in fact Ensley Barton remained to be seen. I realized my hand holding the cup was shaking. I steadied it and sipped.

"Was he at the viewing the other night?"

Without conferring with her sister, Dorothy answered, "Briefly. He left rather suddenly as I recall."

He left suddenly, I thought to myself, to put a knife to my throat. He must have spotted me inside the funeral home.

Lilith jumped in, "A few months ago Ensley had a business proposal he approached Malcolm about. I believe he wanted Malcolm to finance it. Our brother was generous with his wealth. I don't know the particulars but they had a disagreement about matters and never spoke to each other again."

Dorothy sighed, "You know what they say about friends and business."

I wanted to jump off the couch and race over to Matthew's. My legs were twitching with a new found eagerness. I sipped my tea and gazed up at the clock on the wall.

"Is that the time," I asked placing my cup down on the table. "I must be going, lots to do today. Anyhow I recommend filling out the change of address form and mailing it to the post office and they will get Malcolm's mail forwarded."

The sisters thanked me and walked me out.

"Retiring soon are you," one of them asked as I was out the front door.

I guessed it was Dorothy.

CHAPTER 16.

A Pat on the Back Is 18 Inches Away

From.........

At a quarter to seven that evening, I stood in front of Matthew in the loft. My shoulders were back and my face beamed. It didn't really matter because he didn't notice. He was seated on the couch opening a duffle bag that was in the center of the wheel top. He was placing a few items into it. I reported in full detail my conversation with the sisters. When I was done I awaited a compliment on my findings.

There wasn't one.

I watched Matthew shove three different size screwdrivers into the bag. He looked up at me and then back down at the bag. Shoving a roll of duct tape into it he looked up again and asked, "What?"

My shoulders went up an inch and dropped. "I don't know, maybe a compliment on my investigation would be nice."

"Dennis, I hope tomorrow I can give you some applause. Tonight, if we botch this situation, plastic explosives may be dispersed God knows where. I'm not sure I'd be able to track all of them down. That's why we are taking an offensive approach to this thing!"

Well I had to admit, he was determined. I must have been kidding myself; this was no time for personal acknowledgement.

"Dennis," his voice was calmer, "relax."

Raising his left arm he wiggled it until the sleeve slid down, revealing his wrist watch. His eyes gazed at it and his arm dropped.

"Ten minutes to seven," he announced, 'Sandra should be here soon."

He aggressively zipped the duffle bag shut and retreated to the rear of the loft. I decided to sit. When he reappeared he was wearing the black overcoat he wore the night he invaded Everest's house. The same night he removed something that he'd been staring at under a microscope all week.

My stomach shifted as I looked up to see Sandra in a black jacket, her right arm raised in the air. Her fist was clenched as she declared, "Let's rock!"

Matthew smiled.

I fought the urge not to vomit.

"Let's do just that," Matt said scooping up the duffle bag.

Before I knew it we were in our familiar seats in Sandra's car. The closer we got to Russo's Manufacturer's, the more my stomach revolved. The realization of all this was clear as day. We were going to encounter some dangerous people. How were we going to pull this off?

Once again the car rolled on as residential became industrial. Sandra squared the block that the soulless structure of the Russo factory was on. The same pick up truck with the same vanity plates was parked in the same place. Around back the same cargo van was backed up to the same docking bay. Going around the block once more Sandra parked on the street that faced the rear of Russo's and down the block a bit. In the darkness we were hidden. I could see the front of the cargo van.

We all stepped out of the car. The street was a cold corridor of concrete that seemed to repulse the moon light above. Darkness never had a better companion than this patch of ground. I could barely see Matthew as he turned toward me.

"Stay with the car Dennis," he was practically whispering. "Sandra and I will be right back."

I thought to myself, "No argument here."

They walked toward the rear of the factory. Squinting I could barely make out their dark figures. They stopped short of the cargo van and remained in close proximity of each other. After a minute they returned.

Sandra was first to report, "There's no one with the van but there's a light showing beyond the rear door of the building. It seems to be open."

Matthew added, "It appears they haven't loaded anything yet. We need to get inside and conceal ourselves. Time hasn't permitted us the luxury of seeing the layout of this place. I can only assume that there will be boxes or shipping supplies inside. We'll need to use that for cover."

Fear chilled my blood as I blurted out, "What do you expect us to do in there?"

"Shhhh," they both exclaimed as I realized my voice was a bit loud on the silent street. I thought about the expression Matthew used earlier, silence is golden. I repeated my question in a whisper.

Matthew whispered back, "When I feel you need to know that, I'll be sure to tell you."

Sandra grabbed my arm and started leading me toward the rear of Russo's Manufacturers.

"Come on," she said guiding my body that was supported by legs that felt like jelly. "We've got to get inside before they start loading that van."

The dock that extended off the rear of the building didn't exactly line up with the back doors of the van. It was about four feet off the ground and that was close enough for loading purposes. Sandra flattened her palms on the metal surface and pushed herself up onto the cold extension. I did the same. Angling her body to the left of the backdoor she examined the frame where slithers of light were escaping. Extending her head she placed her left ear against the center of the door and I prayed no one was coming out the other side.

"Nothing," she whispered, "I hear nothing."

Switching to the right side of the door she placed a hand on the knob.

My heart rate increased as she started to pull the steel door open. The light escaped a bit more. She slipped inside. I opened the door a bit wider and followed her.

Inside were lots of boxes piled up high. They were dark brown boxes with no labels or markings on them.

Sandra planted her feet and scanned the immediate area. She had her hair tucked under the knit cap and her jacket made noise when I tapped her on the back of it.

She turned around and her eyes thinned inward, an expression that annoyingly asked, "What?"

I whispered, "Where is he?"

She knew I meant Livingston and whispered back, "I don't know. You think it's wise to have three of us crawling around in here?'

"No," I replied shrugging my shoulders.

"Than zip it," she hushed at me. Her head continued to scan the area. Looking back at me she quietly said, "This way."

We walked left of where we entered. An aisle was formed between the boxes on our right and the sheet rocked wall on our left. We followed it until we came to another wall and had to turn right. Crates were stacked up high. We continued our walk and then... there it was.

Voices.

CHAPTER 17.

Fear Factory

"This was my brain child, my creation and you go behind my back like this?" The voice was raised in anger.

There was a space between two stacks of crates about three and a half feet wide. Sandra slid between the stacks and I followed.

"I didn't go behind your back," it was a voice different from the first and it was pleading. "Honestly, I just couldn't reach you. It was a no lose situation…and I have your Money. Here. Now."

Sandra placed her back to the crates closest to the voices. I got on my stomach and inched to the edge of the stack. About twenty-five feet in front of me I could see two men. One was about six feet tall and had thinning black hair gelled back over a wide skull. He wore a gray jacket over a black turtle neck that was tucked into dark blue jeans. Black leather boots completed his ensemble. His right hand was gripping the white t-shirt of a balding man who was a foot shorter than him, and sweating profusely.

The tall man continued, "I map out a plan to distribute this stuff in bulk and you risk exposure by selling one of my bombs to a punk gang!"

His voice grew very excited as he went on, "I should have you done with!"

The smaller guy bellowed, "No, you can't. This is my place of business. You need me."

Releasing the clearly nervous man's shirt, the aggressor's right arm dropped to his side. That was when I saw it. There was the patch of blue ink in between his index finger and his thumb.

The Hope Anchor!

It was him, the same guy who held me at knife point outside the funeral home. The man who claimed he saw me run from the home of Malcolm Everest.

Pure disgust filled his voice as he spat out, "Let's get the truck loaded!"

I had to assume that this guy was Ensley Barton, the man that Malcolm's sisters told me about. He was staring at a crate that had a two by four nailed across the facing of it.

"Hey Marty," he called to the other man.

That was it; he identified Martin Russo Jr. who was scurrying over to this determined individual.

"I don't recognize this crate; open it to make sure it's ours."

Russo picked a crowbar off the floor and wrenched it in between the two-by-four and the facing of the crate. Arching his back he used leverage and the piece of lumber sprung loose. A flat sound rang out as it hit the cement floor. Lifting the cover off the crate a sea of styrofoam began to spill out. Reaching delicately inside, Russo removed an item immersed in a plastic wrapping.

I looked closely and inside the clear plastic I recognized the white, cylindrically-shaped device. It resembled the one that went "boom" in Roosevelt Park last night. Matthew was right. This maniac was shipping these explosives to God knows where.

Well, now for the boneheaded moment of the evening.

The two of them began to pick up the crate cover when the hard rock guitar sound that served as the ring tone for my cell phone went off.

The heads on these two jokers whipped around so fast I inched mine back behind the crate that was hiding me.

Nervously seizing the phone my thumb panicked across the device in an effort to stop it. I did.

"What was that," one of the voices called out.

Sandra had her back to the crate, but her eyes were dissecting me.

"I'm surprised you didn't answer it," she said getting into a crouching position.

"Someone's here," the Australian voice shouted. "This is your fault. We've been exposed by your stupidity."

"No, no," Russo pleaded, "I checked the place before you arrived. No one's here."

"Do you mind telling me what that infernal noise was?"

The question didn't get answered because I heard footsteps coming in my direction. I just knew it was those hard leather boots on the concrete floor. This was the tricky part, should I wait for this guy to find me or should I just bolt? I looked to Sandra to see what she had in mind.

Her left shoulder was placed against the stack of crates. Her right leg was extended outward.

It was sooner than later when the tall man peered around the crates I was hiding behind.

"You again!"

CHAPTER 18.

The Girl, the Maniac, the Weasel, and I

I looked up to see the wide forehead complete with bulging eyeballs. I had pretty much written myself off until I heard a crashing noise.

Sandra threw her shoulder into the stack of crates and they tipped. This guy had his sites set on me and never saw the section that landed right on top of him. I stood up and followed her. She turned left toward the back door.

She stopped suddenly with me on her heels. Russo was blocking our way. He stood there with that crowbar in his right hand. He methodically pounded it into his upturned left palm.

Spinning on her heels, Sandra pushed me in the opposite direction. We found ourselves deeper in the building. I could hear noise behind us. It appeared our Australian friend was emerging from under the crates, accompanied by a mouth full of foul language.

Sandra stopped again and surveyed the room. There was a set of swinging doors. A dim light was behind those doors. Sandra was in front of me when Russo rounded the corner of crates and stopped. He pounded the crowbar again which led me to believe he was nervous about using it. I didn't want to take a chance. Before I could think about it any longer, his partner in crime appeared. Russo was to my right, the Australian to my left, and Sandra straight in front of me. The two of them began to close in on her. Russo raised the crowbar high.

She had them read perfectly. As they converged with her in between she turned and tucked her left shoulder and dropped to the floor. Forward rolling she sprang up on her feet facing me. I watched Russo clip his partner with the crowbar. Wow was he furious!

They squabbled over it for a few seconds but that was all I got to see. Sandra pushed me through the swinging doors.

My eyes adjusted to the dim lighting and I realized we were in a room that didn't look much different from our school's biology classroom. There were rows of stone counters, with a few sinks in the middle of each. On the rear wall were two metal shelves. Glass jars with labels lined each shelf. We ran in that direction. Simultaneous we placed our backs to the shelves keeping enough distance between our pursuers and ourselves.

The doors swung open and it was the Australian who entered first. He started in our direction, hunching forward, propelled by sheer anger.

"You're finished," he shouted pointing at me.

Sandra grabbed a jar off the shelf that contained a gray clay-like substance. She rocketed it toward him. I couldn't tell in the dim light where it hit, but he was clutching his head as an agonizing scream rang out. He probably never saw it coming.

Sandra never gave him a chance. She grabbed another jar and fired it at him. I got in on the action and whipped one at him, but he ducked. Russo, who was coming through the doors, caught it right on the chin.

Smash!

I nailed him. Looking next to me Sandra had another jar in her hand. She double clutched and I saw a chalky white substance in the jar shimmer about. She let it fly and it crashed against the far wall, decorating it in a splash of white.

I grabbed a jar that had something swishing around inside and I sent it spiraling forward. The Australian was just straightening up and it clipped him on his left shoulder. He doubled over and I could see past him. Russo was cowering with blood spurting from his chin.

"Run," Sandra ordered and I did just that, heading toward the wall on my left. I glanced behind me and saw the tall man on the move in our direction.

Sandra ran halfway toward me and stopped and did an about face. The big man turned into our aisle. His teeth were clenched and his face red with anguish.

Sandra acted!

Grabbing the first shelf up high she yanked it down, dropping it right on him. Glass shattered; metal caught flesh and the big man was brought down.

We still had to get out of here and the sweaty bald man was blocking the swinging doors. He looked nervous and scared as we approached him. We couldn't stall for I didn't know how long our other friend would be imprisoned beneath the metal shelf.

"Step aside Russo," I said, masking my fear quite well.

"How... how do you know who I am?"

"Okay Junior," Sandra said angling toward him. "You heard him, step aside."

A defensive look crossed his face and he turned to face Sandra, leaving himself wide open. I took the opportunity and projected my right foot into his left kneecap. He dropped.

His hands were grabbing at me as I tried to step around him. Sandra decided to do some kicking of her own.

Russo gave up and Sandra and I stepped over him. We each had a hand on the swinging doors to freedom when we heard, "Move and I'll shoot."

He emerged from under the metal wreckage with an ominous black firearm in his right fist. He moved quickly coming up behind us. Russo began to get to his feet as well.

"I don't know what you're up to but you're not interfering with my plans," he barked still pointing the weapon.

"That way," he ordered waving the gun in the direction of the swinging doors.

Russo, who was up, held them open as Sandra and I passed through. We were back where we came from.

The crate was still there with the top pried off it and the styrofoam spilled on the floor.

"Now I'm going to be done with you."

"Good idea," Russo added.

"No," the Australian replied, accent and all, "that includes you!"

"What," Russo shouted in protest.

"You screwed this whole thing up. I'm not taking any more chances. He raised the gun and it was about eight inches away from Russo's face.

"Drop it Ensley!"

All heads turned in the direction of the voice. Standing stone-like atop a stack of crates, peering down on us, was Matthew Livingston.

CHAPTER 19.

"BOMBS AWAY!"

Looking up I could see black leather shoes, perfectly creased pants and the black pullover. His eyes were oval piercing instruments aimed at the armed individual.

"Who do you think you are," Ensley replied and I could hear the Australian accent completely. He did some job hiding it that night outside the funeral home.

All the color had drained out of Russo's face as he begged, "Shoot him Ensley, shoot him." He was panic stricken at the site of Livingston.

"I'm going to shoot you first for attracting all this unnecessary attention. It was you who..."

"Drop the gun," Matthew overshot the volume of Ensley's voice.

Ensley didn't budge. He briefly smiled, but didn't budge.

"I don't think you're in a position to make demands," he replied in Matthew's direction.

Matthew's right hand emerged from behind his back he raised it slowly. Clenched in his fist was a white plastic cylindrically-shaped item that I recognized. In his left hand was a small black item that resembled a car keychain remote control.

Ensley's jaw fell slack. His hand holding the gun began to shake. I looked at Russo and he was falling to pieces. Tears streamed down his eyes.

"Where did you get that," Ensley shouted with an unstable voice.

"That crate right next to you."

"Kid," Russo stammered, "put it down. You don't know what you're dealing with."

"Sure I do," Matt replied acting coy. "Story is all over town that you've got these things for sale by the dozen."

"You see you idiot," Ensley started to scream at Russo.

"Drop the gun and I'll put this down."

"Not a chance," he replied still clenching the gun even tighter. "You set that off and you're gone as well."

Matthew was smiling, "Is that supposed to be a selling point? The truth is I missed the fireworks last night at Roosevelt Park. Decided I would make my own. Last chance, drop the gun."

Ensley intensified his grip on the weapon.

"Last chance for you," his accent was icy, "drop the bomb!"

"Dropping it right on you," Matthew said quickly launching it in our direction.

My body retracted in pure terror. I knew Livingston was crazy, but this was beyond the levels of insanity. The white, plastic item spiraled downward, picking up speed. A high pitched wail, which resembled the voice of a young girl, came from Russo. Ensley's eyes were bulging as he completely froze and Sandra....

Wait a second! Sandra showed no sign of fear. She dove at Ensley who looked like a deer caught in a car's headlights. With very little effort she disarmed him. He didn't even notice as the plastic device was hitting the floor.

My hands grasped my ears, Russo cowered, and Ensley dropped to his knees. There was no explosion, no blinding light. The only sound came from Sandra Small who commanded, "Face down on the floor, now!"

She had the gun trained on Ensley and Russo. I looked up at the crates and Matthew was gone. He appeared behind me. Carrying his duffle bag, he walked over to Sandra and handed her the black remote saying, "Thanks."

"Don't mention it," she replied still keeping our friends pinned down.

I exhaled, hard. Wow. I think my life flashed before my eyes, but the problem was, it wasn't that interesting. It dawned on me that Matthew just played a hard core game of chicken with this maniac, and won.

Ensley was face down on the floor, barking foul mouthed complaints towards Matthew, Russo, and me in particular. After his over weight remark I picked up the two-by-four that was still lying on the floor. I whacked him on the back of his head and the verbal onslaught ended. I placed my foot on his back and raised the two-by-four and said to Matthew, who was rifling through his duffle bag, "Silence is golden!"

He removed the roll of metallic adhesive replying, "Duct tape is silver." He tossed it in my direction and said, "Bind him."

I wrapped it around Ensley's wrists and ankles and did the same to Russo.

A pounding noise was heard on the side door. It was accompanied by a gruff voice calling, "Open up!'

"Who's that," I asked.

"The police," Matt responded.

"How do you know?"

"Because I called them," he replied with his eyes pinned on the side door.

CHAPTER 20.

YOU WOULDN'T BELIEVE IT IF I TOLD YOU

As if you had to guess who was on the other side of the door when I opened it. There stood two faces only a mother could love, Detectives' Riley and Withers. Again they wore identical suits. Their faces dropped at the site of me.

Riley, with that head of his that still looked like it was carved out of butter asked, "Did you call us? Is this the anonymous tip?"

I started to relive the fears that I had when I first encountered them, but Matthew didn't let me linger long.

"No," he called out. "That was me who placed that call telling you to be here at exactly this time."

"Is this some kind of a prank," Withers asked, "because I'll drag y'all in this time."

"Oh don't bother," Matthew replied, "we've provided something for you to drag in." He pointed at the two individuals on the floor who were now bound in duct tape.

The two Detectives were trying to take it all in when Matthew continued.

"This is Martin Russo Jr. and this is Mr. Ensley Barton." He pointed at each of them as he said their names. "These two gentlemen have manufactured many plastic explosives including the one that went off in Roosevelt park last night. There are several crates full in the rear of this building in addition to the one that is open."

Silence fell.

Riley was in a crouching position near the crate examining one of the bombs.

Sandra had placed the gun on the floor and said to Whithers, "This is Mr. Barton's gun, I relieved him of it." Withers retrieved it while Riley continued to examine the explosive. His face was lined with confusion.

Matthew spoke, "And furthermore…"

Everyone gave him their attention as he was looking down at Ensley.

"Mr. Barton is in fact, the man who murdered Malcolm Everest."

"Come again," Withers asked.

I must have missed a frost warning in the weather report that morning because Riley froze. He finally stood up and said, "Listen kid, you've got some explaining to do." He had his tough guy routine going and Matthew was completely ignoring it.

"How good are you with the descriptions of suspects," Matthew asked Riley.

"I'm a professional," Riley answered, "why?"

"When Dennis Sommers was hauled in as a suspect Monday afternoon do you recall what he was wearing?"

His arms crossed his chest and in an air of arrogance he replied, "Of course I do."

"Describe his sneakers?"

"White and blue, high topped."

Matthew Livingston reached into his duffle bag and pulled out a clear plastic bag that contained my sneakers.

"That would be these, right?"

Riley looked at my feet and saw that I had gray sneakers on today and looked back at the bag. "That's them and what are you getting at?"

He lofted the plastic bag in Riley's direction and the big man uncrossed his arms to catch it. He looked at the sneakers curiously through the plastic bag. Now it was Matthew who stood with his arms crossed.

"What about them," Riley asked holding the bag in the air.

"When Dennis left the police station I noticed a strange color on his sneakers. I examined the bottom of his shoes and discovered lodged in the soles an off-white substance that appeared to be some sort of a plastic binder. Removing a piece of it I examined it further and discovered traces of chemicals. Do you know what C-4 is?"

Riley stepped closer to Matthew and pointing his finger at him replied, "Hey kid, I spent three years in the military. Don't ask me what C-4 is."

Matt didn't budge, "Three years, I guess that explains your haircut but did you get a free t-shirt with it?"

Riley was about to boil over when Matthew continued, "You know that C-4 is composed of about ninety per cent cyclonite, one of a few chemicals I discovered on this substance. Being a military man you'll also know that the white plastic binder in C-4, after being treated with a solvent and dried can be shaped into any form. In this case it was shaped into the form of a tooth, a dental implant bonded in Malcolm Everest's mouth."

Sandra and I glanced at each other and then at Matthew. This was an all time strange for him. It was then that I suddenly remembered that during this whole ordeal, whenever I was at the loft he was gazing in a microscope or playing with test tubes. He had been studying this the whole time.

"This man's name is Ensley Barton," Matthew continued. "Malcolm Everest has known him for many years and was a long time friend of Ensley's father."

Barton started to stir. His head shook a bit and he was fighting against his bindings as he started to yell, "Cut me loose, will you, I haven't done…"

"Shut up," Withers barked at him.

"Let me help," Sandra said ripping off a piece of duct tape and securing it across Barton's mouth.

"Mr. Dennis Sommers learned just this afternoon that Malcolm and Ensley had a falling out over a business matter that Ensley presented to him. I'll make an assumption that Mr. Barton proposed this whole explosive scheme to Malcolm Everest and he was opposed to the whole thing. Naturally Mr. Barton could not proceed with his plan to manufacture plastic explosives with Malcolm Everest knowing about it. So Mr. Barton removed him."

Matthew stood above Martin Russo Jr. and pointed down at him. Riley and Whithers were waiting in anticipation.

"This is Martin Russo Jr., manufacturer of dental implants, false teeth, bridges, and etcetera. He is Mr. Barton's business partner. He supplied the lab and the ingredients to create these explosives. As we learned, Mr. Barton and Malcom Everest were close at one time. Mr. Barton easily learned that Malcom Everest was due to have dental implants inserted. When Everest's dentist requested an implant be made for his patient, Martin Russo and Ensley Barton created one that could be detonated."

Ensley Barton's bound feet were kicking at the floor in protest.

"A plastic explosive dental implant," Riley whispered in amazement. He looked down at Barton and then over at Russo.

"It was his idea," Russo panicked nodding his head at Barton. "He arranged everything."

"Call the bomb squad," Riley said to Withers, "and get a supervisor on the scene!"

He clutched the bag with the sneakers and looked around the room.

"Send them for your own lab analysis and I assure you you'll get the same results," Matthew said walking toward the back door. I followed and Riley quickly walked behind us.

"What was with the gas situation, the fireplace and all?"

"A cover up," Matthew said raising and dropping his shoulders. He looked at me to finish it.

"I attended Malcolm Everest's wake. Afterward I was grabbed from behind and had a knife placed to my throat. A man's voice told me that he saw me leaving Malcolm's house the day of the explosion and that he better not see me again. I couldn't see my attacker, but the tattoo on his right hand was real clear to me. The same tattoo on his hand," I said pointing to Ensley Barton.

Sandra joined us and Matthew said, "He saw Dennis leaving the house because he was inside moments before to turn on the gas and then detonate the explosive. Real clever, he duped you into thinking that it was a gas explosion. He's an intelligent one. Gas is lighter than air. It will rise and collect in pockets of a room. A detonator must have been either in possession of Mr. Barton or disguised somewhere in the house, most likely something commonly pressed, like a key on a computer keyboard. When the explosive in Everest's mouth went off it ignited these gases that were in the room, making the whole thing resemble a gas explosion. I imagine there was charring or burning on the walls?"

Riley nodded his head.

I tried not to laugh, remembering full well that Matthew saw those walls personally.

"The gases, collected high in the room, causing combustion. There was probably an immediate fire, that self extinguished. Its common in small explosions."

Riley bit his lower lip and then asked, "Don't you think he would have smelled the gas and been alarmed?"

"I guess we'll never know. Gas is actually odorless. That smell is an odorant the gas company puts in so you can be warned of escaping gases. I don't know if Mr. Barton was capable of disabling that or not."

Matthew looked around and continued, "Further more, the dentist who installed the implant, Doctor Quinn, knows nothing of this. He is just as much a victim in this matter. And by the way....."

Riley looked at him

"The anonymous call you received, remains anonymous. Understand?"

I could tell by the half guilt-ridden smile on his face that he was more than happy to take the credit for all of this.

"Yeah, sure kid," he replied.

We left via the back door. Once outside Sandra looked over at Matthew and asked, "So Doctor Quinn installed a plastic explosive in Everest's mouth believing it was a dental implant?"

"Yes."

"Going back to him anytime soon for some dental work?"

Her question was swimming in a pool of dark sarcasm.

Climbing off the docking bay we headed to Sandra's car. I could hear sirens in the distance. I felt a big exhale of relief coming on, but I needed to know something first.

"That white substance you were talking about, is that what you removed from Everest's house Monday night?"

In the darkness I could see him nodding his head slightly.

"Then how could you have found it on the bottom of my sneakers five days later?"

We were climbing into Sandra's car and when the doors were closed he said solemnly, "Because I put it there."

"Oh."

I exhaled.

CHAPTER 21.

SHOULD WE GIFT WRAP IT FOR YOU?

It was Sunday and it almost seemed as if the bright afternoon was trying to relax me with its warmth. After the events of Saturday night I didn't mind. I decided to visit the Livingston loft and was pleased to find the genius wasn't overly occupied like he was the past week. He seemed to be doing maintenance on his equipment. He pulled a white cloth off an old transistor radio that sat on a shelf in the back of the loft. He began to wipe down his microscope.

I sat on one of the folding chairs and he was on the yellow sofa. The microscope was perched on the wheel top.

"Thanks," I managed to get out.

He didn't look up and continued wiping away.

"For what," he replied, still not looking at me.

"For lots of things. Like looking into this matter, for coming to the rescue, for…"

"When you need to thank me for something, I'll be sure to let you know."

I had a few questions, so I let loose.

"What got you curious about the crime?"

"When I arrived at the police station that night I passed a desk that had an enlarged photograph of the crime scene on it. In the photo, the walls of Everest's computer room were charred black in very high places. I was curious. At the same time, I overheard two Detectives mention that there was an arson expert surveying the scene and he claimed that a gas explosion of some sort was responsible for the death of Malcom Everest. It didn't seem right to me."

"How about the dental implant?"

"While examining the walls of Everest's home I found that compound on the floor. It wasn't charred like other items around it. When I started examining it under a microscope, I wasn't sure if it was part of a denture or part of a plastic explosive. The more I tested it, it appeared to be both. I became suspicious and had you find out who was the dentist of Malcolm Everest. During our dinner with the good dentist I realized that Russo strong armed the contract for Dr. Russo's implant work. Namely by lighting his office on fire. "

I sat in amazement. I began to speak and suddenly Matthew's head snapped up. His eyes enlarged slightly, stretching beyond me. Behind me to be exact.

Now I heard what was alarming him. Lumbering up into the loft was Riley and Withers. Their heads were moving side-to-side like they were watching a tennis match.

"What's the meaning of this," Matthew demanded still clutching the cloth.

Withers asked, "What on earth is this place?"

Matt stared at them fiercely and replied, "Mr. Withers, let me introduce you to a word that originated in the eleven hundreds, warrant!"

He overly pronounced the two syllables of the last word adding to the more severe nature of his message.

"That's Detective Withers," the headstrong police man said.

Matthew, still seated, allowed a momentary smile and said, "When you don't require me to solve your crimes, maybe I'll refer to you as a Detective."

The hush that overcame the room was deafening.

Riley brushed past his partner still taking in the strange surroundings. "We need some answers from you, for instance…"

Matthew interrupted, "According to the news report on the radio the police have breaking news on the mysterious death of Malcolm Everest and two suspects in custody. Perhaps it is I who require questions from you."

"Do we have to haul you in?"

Matthew sent an icy glare towards Riley and replied, "Be my guest. Haul me in and by this evening the press will know how you bungled this one. They'll learn how you almost let someone get away with murder and allowed a shipment of bombs to hit the street."

He smiled. He had them in check mate. He stood up and the Detectives, like myself, could see him and behind him all his test tubes and chemistry paraphernalia.

I believe it was then that they realized they were dealing with a very different kind of seventeen year old.

"Dennis," he called to me, "you must go now. I need to speak to these gentlemen alone."

I left. On the walk home and halfway through dinner that evening I wondered what it was he was going to talk to them about. After the dinner table was cleared my family was paid a visit from the very lovely Detective's Withers and Riley, who furnished a full apology to my parents for hauling me in Monday afternoon. They explained the situation while Withers paid me a few compliments. I was shocked and confused by all of this, but then it was Riley who gave it away. That head that still looked like it was carved out of butter couldn't restrain the sour expression behind his partner's words. I knew then that Matthew Livingston had compromised them somehow. He constrained them to do this. I wanted to laugh when they told my mom what a fine journalist I would be one day.

For once in my life I couldn't wait for Monday morning. Somehow in my mind it got me emotionally further away from the drama we experienced Saturday night. When it finally arrived I made my way to the rear of the school building. I walked over to Sandra who was getting out of her car. We just looked at each other and then broke out into smiles.

"You and Matt gave me some scare."

She laughed heartily for a second and said, "That was the whole idea and I'll say you sure did sell it."

"You're right," I said beginning to laugh myself, "There's no way I could have acted that convincing." The truth of the matter was I thought it was a live explosive that was coming my way. Looking at the rear of the school, I saw the guy who threw it.

Matthew Livingston had his tan jacket on and was carrying a binder and a small text book under his right arm. As he approached us he asked, "Did you receive the dinner guests I sent you last night?"

"Thanks," I said with a guilty smile.

"I heard all about it," Sandra added, "those two are impossible."

"Yeah," Matthew agreed, "but I actually don't mind them."

I thought for a second about Withers and Riley and for once my mind didn't reflect on the incident one week ago in Everest's home. My fear had vanished. Maybe that was what Matt had planned when he got them to apologize to my folks. If it was, I silently thanked him. I would like to know what it is he said to the two of them. Perhaps I'll never know. One thing I did know was that he straightened out my state of mind I was complaining about earlier.

"It's about that time," Sandra announced.

I looked at them for a moment, basking in the morning sun and said, "Yes it is Sandra, thankfully."

We headed toward the rear door of the school. I couldn't help but sense a feeling of gratefulness surrounding the three of us. I believe it was there to stay.

Blogging with Dennis Sommers

After this episode with Matthew Livingston I made a point to not be freaked out by his random knowledge and actually look into some of the things he deduced. For instance, when he recognized the tattoo to be an Australian hope anchor I researched the history of tattooing in Australia and learned the following.

During the nineteenth century, Australia was largely used by Great Britain as a warehouse for British criminals. Convicts made up the majority of the British population in Australia. Transportation took place on freighters with convicts imprisoned below decks. Prisoner's quarters were cramped and confined. The prisoners themselves were often shackled. Quality of life was poor and disease was common. During these transports, many prisoners passed time by tattooing themselves. The hope anchor was a common tattoo that is believed to be derived from a passage in the Bible that referenced hope as an anchor for the soul. Prisoners tattooed an anchor in a downside position and sometimes wrote the initials of a loved one that they *hoped* to return to.